Carter hooked his finger underneath her chin and lifted her head until his eyes met hers. "He must have the most impossible standards on the planet. I cannot imagine you being a disappointment to anyone, Rainey."

Her mouth tipped up in a grin. "He would not approve of that nickname."

Carter's eyes sparkled with laughter. "Then I should probably use it more often."

Cradling her head, he leaned in and met her lips in a slow, gentle kiss that was nothing like Lorraine had expected. Given his personality, she had braced herself for a savage plundering, but Carter surprised her with his tenderness.

She leaned into him, pressing her body flush against his. The heat radiating from every part of him scorched her being, lighting a fire that spread throughout her bloodstream. A soft mewl escaped her throat as Carter's hand traveled down her spine, stopping at the small of her back. He cradled her waist and pulled her even tighter against him.

His tongue traced along the seam of her lips, urging them to part, but when they did he didn't plunge inside. Instead, his assault was just as devastatingly tender, which did more to melt her heart than any fiery kiss ever could. His tongue delved in and out of her mouth, gentle, yet insistent, eliciting a moan that tore from her chest.

Carter emitted a groan of displeasure as he reluctantly ended the kiss, but he didn't release her. He continued to cradle her in his arms, the streetlamp casting a soft glow across his face, illuminating the hunger in his eyes.

Gazing up at him, Lorraine whispered, "What is it about you, Carter Drayson?"

Books by Farrah Rochon

Harlequin Kimani Romance

Huddle with Me Tonight
I'll Catch You
Field of Pleasure
Pleasure Rush
A Forever Kind of Love
Always and Forever
Delectable Desire

FARRAH ROCHON

had dreams of becoming a fashion designer as a teenager, until she discovered she would be expected to wear something other than jeans to work every day. Thankfully, the coffee shop where she writes does not have a dress code.

When Farrah is not penning stories, the avid sports fan feeds her addiction to football by attending New Orleans Saints games.

Delectable Desire

FARRAH ROCHON

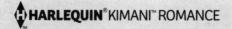
HARLEQUIN® KIMANI™ ROMANCE

For Phyllis Bourne.

No one brainstorms by text message better than you do.

"Wise words bring many benefits, and hard work brings rewards."

—*Proverbs* 12:14

Recycling programs
for this product may
not exist in your area.

ISBN-13: 978-0-373-86306-8

DELECTABLE DESIRE

Copyright © 2013 by Harlequin Books S.A.

For questions and comments about the quality of this book, please contact us at CustomerService@Harlequin.com.

H HARLEQUIN®
™ www.Harlequin.com

Printed in U.S.A.

Dear Reader,

When Kimani invited me to participate in the The Draysons: Sprinkled with Love series, it felt as if I'd hit the lottery. I watched endless episodes of the Food Network's *Cupcake Wars* and had several meetings with a celebrated pastry chef, and was able to call it research! Do you see why I love my job?

All joking aside, researching the world of artisan baking was one of the most fascinating things I have ever done. The artistry, creativity and sheer amount of work that goes into making those elaborate cake creations left me in awe. As I brought my hero, Carter Drayson, to life, my goal was to show that compassion and dedication in everything he did, both in and out of the kitchen.

It is my sincere hope that you enjoy reading *Delectable Desire* as much as I enjoyed writing it. Although, that may require you to eat a cupcake while you read. Ha! As always, I would love, love, love to hear from you. Look me up on Facebook and Twitter, or email me at farrah@farrahrochon.com.

And remember to pick up *Delicious Destiny* by Yahrah St. John next month to see the bakers from Lillian's duke it out in the "You Take the Cake" baking competition!

Sweet reading,

Farrah Rochon

All the thanks in the world to Melissa Samuels of Melissa's Fine Pastries in New Orleans. Your insight into the world of artisan baking was invaluable. And your cakes and pastries are the best! Thank you so much for sharing your talent.

And thanks to my fellow authors in The Draysons: Sprinkled with Love series, A.C. Arthur and Yahrah St. John. You both made this process even sweeter!

Chapter 1

Carter Drayson rubbed his hands together in anticipation as he approached his workstation in the kitchen at Lillian's, his family's bakery. It was stocked with all of the necessary ingredients for his newest creation, a salted-caramel, dark chocolate cake. As he surveyed his supplies, Carter realized he was missing the most important ingredient: flour. He strode over to the pantry where the drums of high-quality cake flour were stored.

He entered the pantry and stopped short.

Instead of flour, Carter discovered a caramel-colored beauty who looked as edible as the cake he was about to make. She crooked her finger.

"Come here, Carter," she whispered in a silky voice.

His mouth went dry as he took a step forward.

"No, Carter, why don't you come this way?"

He whipped around, finding another incredibly hot woman perched on the counter, her dark, smooth thighs crossed. Her breasts were precariously close to spilling out of her low-cut top. She reached over and picked up a sliver of the Belgian chocolate he'd chopped for his cake. She parted her soft, full lips and placed the chocolate on her tongue.

Carter groaned, taking a step toward her.

"Don't go there, Carter. Come here."

He turned to his right and found a *third* woman. This one was honey-colored and, as far as he could tell, completely naked. She had locks of silky, light brown hair flowing down her body, strategically covering all of her luscious girl parts.

He tipped his head to the ceiling and laughed. "This must be heaven."

"Caaaarter," the three women sang.

Carter's gaze shot back to the counter. Miraculously, all three were now perched there, sitting side by side.

And now all three of them were naked.

The dark chocolate beauty picked up a plump strawberry and bit into the tender fruit.

"Do you want a piece of this, Carter?"

"Oh, yeah, baby," he groaned.

His caramel goddess held out a bowl of fluffy whipped cream.

"How about this?" she asked, scooping some up with her finger and sticking it between her lips. Her eyes closed as she ran her tongue up and down her finger, licking it clean.

"You're the cake artist, Carter," Miss Honey said. "Why don't you come over here and show us what you do best?"

This was definitely heaven.

Carter walked—no, more like glided—across the

floor. Dark Chocolate held out the half-eaten straw-berry to him.

As he leaned forward to bite it, the oven's timer went off.

Ding. Ding. Ding.

Wait. That wasn't the oven. It was his phone.

"Nooooo," Carter growled.

His eyes popped open. Just as he'd feared, he was lying in his bed, twisted up in the sheets. He closed his eyes, but it was too late. The dream was gone.

Ding. Ding. Ding.

"Dammit." He reached over and grabbed the phone. "Hello," he bit out.

"Carter, where are you? You were supposed to be here an hour ago."

It was his cousin Belinda. Great. If the incredible dream he'd been in the midst of hadn't already rushed out of his head, it sure as hell would be gone now. Carter peered at the clock on his nightstand. He'd slept right through his alarm.

"Carter, are you still there?"

"I'm here," he said, yawning and stretching.

"Grandma Lillian wants to meet with us. You need to get over here now."

"I'm on my way." He disconnected the call and closed his eyes again, hoping against hope that Dark Chocolate and her ripe, juicy strawberry would reappear, but she wasn't there. Instead, he saw his grandmother frown-ing at him. That instantly iced his smoking-hot dream. And lit a fire under his ass.

Carter hopped out of bed. He grabbed a quick shower, making sure he scrubbed away remnants of the previ-ous night's hard partying.

Last night had been epic, especially for the middle

of the week. He'd complained about having to fly solo now that his best friend and fellow baker at Lillian's, Malik, had gone and gotten himself hooked up with a woman—his cousin Belinda of all people—but Carter was no longer complaining. Not having Malik around meant more women for him, and he'd had no problems collecting phone numbers last night. He had four new ones stored in his cell. Now he just needed to remember which number went with which girl. He knew he should have snapped their pictures last night.

Clean and dressed in slacks and a pressed polo shirt, Carter snatched a banana from the bowl on his kitchen counter as he made his way out of his condo. He sank into the soft leather bucket seat of his Basalt Black Metallic Porsche Panamera—a little something he'd bought himself for his thirtieth birthday—and swiftly made his way through the tree-lined streets of Glenville Heights. He sailed past the Drayson family's gated estate on his way to the Kennedy Expressway. A half hour later, Carter pulled into the garage just off North Michigan Avenue, steps away from the bakery.

His grandparents had been lucky to snatch up this prime real estate on Chicago's famed Magnificent Mile. In fact, they owned the entire building. Various businesses leased the offices on the floors above, but the bottom floor was reserved for Lillian's. Named after his grandmother, Lillian Reynolds-Drayson, who'd first ensnared the taste buds of Chicagoans while working at a local cafeteria, the bakery had a loyal customer base that couldn't get enough of Lillian's sweet treats.

Carter always felt a measure of pride when he thought about how his young, widowed grandmother had made a way for herself and her son, before his grandfather, Henry Drayson, had swept her off her feet. The story of the first time they'd met, and the early days of the bakery, was a staple around the holidays.

Carter entered through the back door. On one side of the hallway was the massive kitchen, which took up a majority of the first floor. The other side housed several offices that were used to conduct bakery business and a storage room for the extra bakeware and packaging materials. The front area comprised the showroom, which faced Michigan Avenue.

As he walked up the hallway, Carter strolled past framed photographs of Lillian's throughout the years, starting with his grandmother holding Uncle Dwight in her arms in front of the modest first storefront on Chicago's South Side, and ending with the family picture they took outside the Michigan Avenue store when Lillian's was featured in a local magazine last year. The rich marble facade of this location was a far cry from the little nondescript building where Lillian's had first gotten its start.

"Carter."

Carter stopped and turned at the sound of his father's voice.

"What's up?" Carter asked.

Devon Drayson did not look as if he was in the mood for exchanging idle chitchat. "Why are you just getting here?" he asked.

"Had a long night," Carter answered with a grin. "Believe me, it was worth walking in an hour late."

"An hour and a half," his father corrected him. "Carter, when are you going to start taking your work seriously?"

His spine straightened in protest. "I do take my work seriously. Do you know how many people come to Lillian's specifically requesting that I design their cakes?

My work brings in more business than anyone else around here."

"I'm not discounting your talent, just your work ethic. You should have been here to open the bakery early this morning, not strolling in hours late as if you don't have a care in the world."

This from the king of the carefree lifestyle. His father had perfected bachelorhood, never even coming close to marrying. Yet he had the nerve to talk about how Carter lived his life?

"I know what it's like to be young and single, but there comes a time when you have to think about the long-term, Carter." His father took a step closer and lowered his voice. "You know that your grandparents will soon let go of the reins of this business. Now, do you want a piece of it?"

Carter was tempted to say no, but that would only cause him more grief. The truth was, he'd been questioning a lot lately whether he still wanted to be a part of the family business.

He had never felt as if he was as much a part of Lillian's as his cousins were, and he placed much of the blame squarely on the shoulders of the man standing before him. After all, it was his father's fault that Carter was the only illegitimate grandchild. As the only bastard of the bunch, Carter had always felt as if he had to work extra hard to prove that he belonged.

His grandparents had never made him feel like an outsider, but Carter knew they didn't approve of his father's perpetual bachelorhood. The fact that his father had never married Carter's mother had been the subject of many disagreements over the years.

But that was his *father's* issue. Carter had nothing

to do with that. He was a part of the bakery's legacy, too, dammit.

"I have as much stake in Lillian's as the others do," Carter said.

"Then start acting like it," his father demanded. "You need to show everyone in this family that you are committed to this business."

"Maybe the family needs to show that they're committed to *me*," he countered, letting the frustration he normally hid behind a carefree smile rise to the surface. "I didn't have the advantage of growing up on the great Drayson Estate the way Belinda and Drake did. I wasn't there every Sunday afternoon like Monica and Shari. Yet I put just as much time into Lillian's as they do. No, I put in more. I bust my ass for this business. So, tell me, Dad, does the family value *my* input? Does everyone here realize just what *I* bring to the table?"

"Don't get full of yourself, Carter. You may be a good baker, but there are others out there. Just because you have Drayson blood running through your veins doesn't mean you get an automatic pass. You need to straighten up, or you're going to find yourself cut out of this business."

With that his father turned and went back into the sales office.

Carter stood in the hallway for several minutes, trying like hell to rein in his fury. He was damned tired of always having to defend himself. From his teenage days, when he'd worked as a delivery boy, to now, as one of the head bakers, he'd given Lillian's one hundred percent of himself. But his best never seemed good enough for his family.

Carter thought about the phone call he'd received last week from a representative of Robinson Restaurants, one of the hottest restaurant conglomerates on the East Coast. The man Carter had spoken to had been extremely interested in Lillian's, and specifically in what Carter had accomplished as the bakery's premier artisan cake designer. When he'd asked if Carter would be interested in becoming the executive pastry chef for the Robinson Restaurants Group's flagship New York location, he had been floored.

The offer had warranted some serious soul searching. He was torn between loyalty to his family's business and the appeal of finally being somewhere where his work was appreciated. Discussions like the one he'd just had with his father did nothing but tip the scales in New York's favor.

Despite what Devon believed, Carter knew there wasn't a damn thing wrong with his work ethic. He put his heart and soul into Lillian's, pulling sixty-hour workweeks, spending his time off at home working on his decorating technique. He loved this business, but he wasn't sure the feeling was mutual.

Oh, he had no doubts his family loved him, but did they *value* him? Maybe it would take his leaving to show them just how much he was worth to Lillian's.

The emergency meeting for which his grandmother had summoned the Drayson grandchildren turned out to be a slightly beefed-up version of their normal weekly status report, with the exception of a more in-depth discussion of Lillian's involvement in *You Take the Cake,* a reality TV show their family had agreed to participate in. His aunt Daisy had flown to Los Angeles to meet with the show's producers and sign the contract. Lillian's was officially on board.

Unfortunately, so was Brown Sugar Bakery, owned

and operated by onetime Lillian's employee and ultimate backstabber Dina English. Dina was a four-letter word in more ways than one around this kitchen. Carter was personally looking forward to annihilating Brown Sugar Bakery on national television. He could only hope there would be tears involved.

After the meeting, his younger cousin Shari approached him. Like the rest of the Drayson clan, Shari had come up in the ranks at the bakery. She, too, specialized in cakes, along with Lillian's ever-popular gourmet cupcakes.

"Have you finalized the details for the event at Lincoln Park Zoo?" Shari asked.

Carter nodded. "We're providing four cakes in all. A Bengal tiger, a silverback gorilla, a giraffe and a Nicobar pigeon. One of my former classmates is loaning me a few of his students from the culinary school he just opened. We're going to transport the tiger, gorilla and pigeon, but the giraffe will have to be constructed on-site."

"Sounds as if you have everything under control."

"I always have things under control," Carter snapped, grimacing at the unwarranted bite in his tone. He blamed the earlier conversation with his dad for his irritability.

Shari eyed him curiously. "Maybe you should lay off the clubbing and get more sleep at night. You'd be in a better mood."

Carter let her remark pass. It was no mystery to his cousins that he liked to have a good time, and he made no apologies. He was young, single and financially set for life thanks to his family's business. And, according to popular opinion, he wasn't hard on the eyes, either. Why the hell shouldn't he get out there and enjoy himself?

He took a cursory tour around the kitchen, making sure everything was going according to schedule. They had several big orders to get out today, including a cake for an event being hosted by the mayor's office. Lillian's most important asset was its reputation, and Carter made it his business to make sure every dessert that left this kitchen lived up to his grandmother's incredibly high standards.

Amber Mitchell, one of their assistant bakers who doubled as the receptionist, rounded the corner. "Carter, there's a guy out front who needs to speak to someone about setting up an event tasting. Belinda and Drake are both busy with other customers. Can you talk to him?"

"Does this guy have a name?" he asked Amber, who'd turned her attention to a cake that was ready to be frosted.

She hunched her shoulders. "Probably. He's in a three-piece suit and is wearing an awful toupee."

"That helps," he drawled.

Carter headed for the retail area. The hard work happened behind the scenes in the kitchen, but it was the storefront that truly awed the bakery's customers. The opulent, yet tasteful, decor was just one of the things that made the name Lillian's synonymous with class and sophistication.

Gilding burnished the rich mahogany woodwork, sparkling under the illumination of crystal chandeliers. The polished marble countertops that were inlaid with ribbons of copper and gold made a statement about Lillian's long history of catering to Chicago's elite.

Sunlight streamed in from the huge windows that faced North Michigan Avenue. Nestled inside the bay windows were displays of lavishly decorated cakes and delectable desserts. They had discovered over the years that showcasing the bakery's products was, by far, the most effective way to entice patrons to step inside the store's welcoming glass doors.

Carter spotted the gentleman in the three-piece suit. He was peering into the custom-made glass display case that ran the width of the store.

"Carter Drayson," he greeted, holding out a hand. "How can I help you?"

The man returned the handshake. "Lowell Thompson. I'm a client of Bowen and Associates on the third floor. Howard Bowen recommended Lillian's for an event my company is sponsoring next month."

"Howard is a very good customer."

"He tells me Lillian's sells the best desserts around. I'm new to Chicago, so I'm still learning my way."

"Well, let me give you the most delicious tour you'll ever take in this city."

Carter retrieved a small silver platter from behind the counter and picked out several sweets from the array of intricately decorated cupcakes, pies and Lillian's famous petit fours.

As Lowell Thompson sampled a dark chocolate espresso cupcake, Carter explained that nearly every item could be made in miniature sizes, more suitable to cocktail parties and other catered events.

"You have an impressive operation going here," the man commented.

"It's been going for several decades, and it just keeps growing. These are our newest bestsellers." Carter motioned to the shelves lined with Lillian's latest hot item: ingredients for their most popular cookie and brownie flavors in prepackaged mixes that customers could bake at home. It had been his cousin Shari's idea, and it was turning out to be a lucrative one. Even so, most of their customers claimed that no matter how hard they tried, the make-at-home desserts didn't have that special Lillian's touch.

"I'm running late for a meeting, but if you have some time later this afternoon, I'd like to return and discuss a few options."

"Absolutely." Carter retrieved a business card from his pocket. "Why don't you log on to our website and look over our product offerings? If there's something special you're seeking, just let me know. We'll work with you."

Carter bade the man goodbye and turned back toward the kitchen, but he stopped short at the sight of a woman standing at the register talking to his cousin Drake. He'd never seen her in the bakery before. His gaze traveled over her soft yellow skirt and matching silk blouse, taking in every nuance. Even though the clothes were a bit stuffy for Carter's taste, he had to admit that she wore them well. Damn well.

She was petite—couldn't top more than five feet— with milky, caramel-colored skin and luxuriant light brown hair streaked with honey-colored highlights. She was what his grandmother would call a classic beauty.

And she came from money. No doubt about it.

Her clothes said it, but the bling in her ears and around her wrist practically screamed it.

After less than a minute of observing her, Carter had already sized her up. He could tell the kind of person she was simply by the way she held herself: regal, untouchable. Not his usual type of woman—the exact opposite, in fact. His usual type wore about eighty percent less clothing. But there was something about this one that made him want to ruffle her feathers.

Carter started for the counter, but halted as a mother

who'd been picking out pastries with her young son cut him off. The little boy, who was holding a cupcake, walked smack into Ms. Prim and Proper, smearing icing all over the designer jacket she held draped over her arm.

Carter stood back and waited for the fireworks.

"Oh, I'm so sorry!" the mother exclaimed, grabbing the mushed cupcake from the boy's hand.

Prim and Proper lifted the jacket to eye level, regarded the offending stain…and licked it.

Carter's head jerked back.

"Mmm. That's pretty good. I see why my jacket wanted a taste," she said, smiling down at the little boy, who giggled in return. "But it looks as if you need a new cupcake." She motioned for Drake to give the little boy another one.

Shock rooted Carter where he stood. That wasn't the reaction he'd been expecting. Neither had he expected a simple smile to transform her from reserved to…approachable. Very approachable.

Carter sidled up to the counter where she'd redirected her attention to Drake and a cake brochure she'd apparently brought in from one of their competitors.

"You made the right choice," Carter said, motioning to the brochure.

She turned to him. "Excuse me?"

"The cakes here at Lillian's are a thousand times better than what you'll get over there." He extended his hand. "Carter Drayson, one of the head pastry chefs. And you are?"

She hesitated for the merest moment before accepting his outstretched hand. Carter's initial suspicion was confirmed: she definitely came from money. No way had this smooth palm ever engaged in a millisecond of physical labor.

"Lorraine," she replied.

"It's my deepest pleasure to meet you, Lorraine." He executed a short bow. "Welcome to Lillian's."

"You mind, Carter?" This from Drake. "I'm trying to help Lorraine with her order."

"What's the occasion?" Carter asked. "Birthday?"

"Wedding shower," Drake answered.

Disappointment shot through him. Well, that was fun while it lasted.

"My sister's wedding shower," Lorraine interjected.

Carter's radar immediately went on high alert. She had been pretty quick to clarify that bit of information, and wasn't *that* interesting as hell?

Deciding to temporarily dismiss the fact that Lorraine wasn't his usual type, Carter retrieved the sample brochure from his cousin's hand, earning an annoyed look from Drake.

"Nothing you'll find at this place will be good enough," he continued as he examined the brochure. He glanced at Drake, whose stare was downright murderous. As if Carter cared. His morning had suddenly taken an interesting twist. He needed to know whether there was something more lurking underneath Miss Prim and Proper's stuffy outfit.

Although Carter still wasn't sure why. She wasn't his type. Was she? No, she definitely wasn't his type.

Yet he felt the smile he normally invoked only when he was going in for the kill draw across his face.

"Your sister's wedding shower deserves something more than a generic cake," he continued. "Although even the generic cakes at Lillian's are much better than anything else you'll find in this city."

"Carter, don't you have somewhere else to be?" Drake bit out.

"As a matter of fact, I do. In my office with Lorraine here. I think we need to put our heads together and come up with something extra special for your sister's wedding shower." He tossed the brochure in the trash behind the counter and motioned to Lorraine. "Follow me."

She looked from him to Drake and then back at him.

"Come on." Carter gestured. "It'll be painless, I promise."

Two well-arched eyebrows peaked over her expressive brown eyes. She directed her question to Drake. "Is it safe to follow him back there?"

"Depends on who you ask" was his cousin's answer before turning his attention to another customer who had just walked through the door.

Carter led her down the hallway and into one of the two offices used for customer consultations. He offered her a seat before retrieving an order form from the cherry filing cabinet.

"So, what's the theme of the shower?" he started.

"I'm not sure we've established a theme, per se. It will be your typical bridal shower."

"What can you tell me about your sister? What are some of her hobbies?"

Lorraine's shoulders stiffened defensively. "Why do you need to know about Trina's hobbies?"

"So we'll know what kind of cake would work best for her wedding shower."

"I don't understand. It is just a cake," she said.

"Lorraine, Lorraine, Lorraine." Carter shook his head. "There is no such thing as just a cake. Not here at Lillian's."

The smooth skin on her forehead creased in a dubious frown.

Damn, she was cute. Still not his type, but cute.

"Where is the shower being held?" he asked.

"The tearoom at the Drake Hotel."

"Nice," Carter said. "Sophisticated."

She choked out a laugh; it transformed her entire expression.

"What, is your sister not nice?" he asked.

"My sister is one of the nicest people I know. But she is definitely not stuffy and sophisticated. If I were to ask Trina's opinion, I suspect she would choose a nice Irish pub or even a sports bar to hold her bridal shower. However, stronger forces prevail."

"So she's into sports?"

Lorraine nodded. "Sports, and the outdoors. She has always been the athletic twin."

"You're twins?" Another tidbit revealed.

"I didn't mention that? Yes, Trina is my twin sister. We are fraternal, but the fact that we are twins is unmistakable."

"So she's beautiful and she's into outdoor activities," Carter commented.

An instant blush blossomed on Lorraine's cheeks. "Thank you," she said. "That is very sweet of you."

"I bake cakes for a living. I can't help being sweet," he said, adding a deliberate dose of flirtation to his grin.

Lorraine's eyes lit with amusement. "Do you practice these lines, or do they come naturally?"

Carter's grin widened. "It's natural." He was having way more fun than he usually did during a cake consultation.

"I can tell," she said. "You are a natural-born flirt." She crossed her ankles in that proper way his aunt Daisy sat, and folded her hands on her knee. "So, what do you need to know about Trina?"

Carter glanced down at the form on the desk. He *was*

supposed to be working, wasn't he? "You said she's into outdoor activities. What's her favorite?"

"Scuba diving. Much to my parents' chagrin. They are both afraid she will eventually drown, or be bitten by a shark, or some other such nonsense."

Carter snapped his fingers. "What about a deep-sea-themed bridal shower?"

Her frown returned, her expression becoming even more uncertain than before. "You don't know my mother," she said. "I doubt she would go for Little Mermaid party hats."

"Think seashells sprinkled with diamond dust and live coral centerpieces." Carter spun away from his desk and went over to one of the bookcases lining the wall. He pulled down a binder from two years ago, and flipped to June, finding pictures of a cake he'd made for a birthday party that had rivaled most wedding cakes. Ironically, the party did have Disney's *The Little Mermaid* as the overriding theme, but the "Under the Sea" cake he'd made had been much more refined.

He took the chair opposite Lorraine's and spread the binder out across his lap, turning it so it faced her.

"Goodness," she breathed. "That is gorgeous."

"It's one of my favorite cakes," Carter said, feeling the surge of pride that always surfaced when talking about his creations. This one had put him into another stratosphere in the cake-making world. It had taken a full twelve hours to decorate, and that was after he had spent several days crafting seashells, sea horses, starfish and other ocean creatures out of gum paste.

"I could make the colors softer, and add edible glitter to make it more elegant," Carter continued.

She studied the pictures for several minutes, flipping through the pages to view the pictures he'd taken from every angle. "It *is* beautiful," she mused. "But everyone will be expecting a traditional cake."

"So, why not defy expectations? Pardon the pun, but can you imagine the splash something like this would make? In my opinion, this is much more worthy of the Drake than your run-of-the-mill tiered cake."

Carter could see the indecision flickering across her features, and was afraid he'd gone too far with the hard sell. A smidgen of self-reproach attacked his conscience, because he suddenly realized that he wasn't thinking as much about selling a cake as he was thinking about selling himself. To her. He wanted to wow her with his skills.

"You don't have to make the decision right now," Carter said, backing off a bit. "Why don't you take a day to think it over? You can call tomorrow and let me know what you decide."

Still studying the pictures, she shook her head and said, "I don't need any more time. I've already made my decision." She sat upright and gave him a firm nod. "I want this cake."

"You sure?" Carter asked. "Really, you can take your time."

"No. I want it just as you described it, with the softer colors and the shimmering glitter. I want it to look like an enchanted underwater fantasy."

"Well, if you're sure, we can put the order in now. You'll just have to put twenty percent down."

She opened the snap on the designer clutch she held in her lap and pulled out several hundred-dollar bills. "How much is the deposit?"

"That will depend on the size of the cake, and on the extent of the work that will need to be done. Let me get a bit more information from you, and then we'll work up a price."

Her eagerness was laced with something else, a certain resolve that shouldn't come from simply ordering a cake. He worked up her order and gave her the invoice. Instead of putting down a deposit, she paid for the eighteen-hundred-dollar cake in full. In cash. That was something he didn't see every day.

After they'd concluded their meeting, Carter walked her out of the office and back to the showroom.

Lorraine held out her hand to him. "Thank you so much for your help," she said. "I cannot believe it took a stranger to help me come up with the perfect theme for my own twin's wedding shower, but I am very grateful you did. Trina is going to love this."

"Happy I could help," Carter said, still holding on to her soft hand. He had no desire to let it go anytime soon. He slipped his hand into his left pocket and pulled out one of his business cards, handing it to her. "If you need anything else, don't hesitate to call me. Anytime."

She smiled. Damn, her smile was nice.

"Thank you, Carter."

And with that, she was gone.

For a few moments Carter contemplated following her, but after coming in over an hour late this morning, he knew better than to leave the bakery.

His thoughts stretched back to the conversation he'd had with his dad earlier, and Carter acknowledged what he had to do. His cousins already had an unfair advantage over him when it came to Lillian's. It was time he proved to this family once and for all just what he was worth to them…even if he might not be working here for much longer.

Chapter 2

As she exited the bakery, Lorraine slipped on her Roberto Cavalli sunglasses and headed up Michigan Avenue. She couldn't risk walking any faster than a casual stroll; her heart was already beating triple time.

She had not been prepared for the likes of Carter Drayson.

Her hand still tingled from their parting handshake. His fingers were long, the skin slightly rough, with a couple of darker spots, as if he'd been burned by a hot cake pan a time or two.

And he was gorgeous. Seriously, unquestionably gorgeous.

From the moment he'd stepped up to the counter and introduced himself, Lorraine had been aware of every breath that had left her lungs, because it had been just that hard to breathe around him. It wasn't the first time she'd been immediately bowled over by a charming guy, but it had never been that intense. His silky voice, vibrant smile and overpowering charisma had hit her like a Midwestern tornado in the middle of the active season.

"He's probably just as dangerous, too," she said underneath her breath. Best to stay far, far away from Lillian's. She didn't need the extra calories from their sinfully tempting desserts, and she most certainly did not need the devastating Carter laying on the heavy charm.

Lorraine arrived at the garage where she'd parked her car and took the elevator to the fifth level. Even though she lived within walking distance, she'd driven to the bakery because Lillian's was just the first stop on a slew of errands she had to run for the shower preparations.

It had practically taken an act of Congress to convince the family driver, Bradford, that she didn't need to be chauffeured today. Driving her own car was one freedom that Lorraine refused to relinquish. It gave her the illusion that she had some control over her own life; it was hard to keep a low profile when you were driven around in a gleaming pearl-white Bentley. She had a hard enough time distancing herself from her famous last name; she didn't need the "look at me" car attracting the curious gazes of onlookers.

Lorraine was convinced that her name had had nothing to do with the attention Carter had given her. Oh, he'd flirted—she had pegged him as a natural-born player from the minute he'd sidled up to the counter—but it wasn't because he'd recognized her as a Hawthorne-Hayes.

It had been…nice. Refreshing.

She'd spent her entire twenty-five years bearing that name, and although being an heir to one of the wealthiest families in Chicago had its perks, it was definitely not all it was cracked up to be.

Lorraine slipped behind the wheel of her Jaguar. She loved this car. It was luxurious, but not overly so. It certainly didn't raise as many eyebrows as the Bentley did.

She turned over the ignition, then immediately shut the car off.

"What were you thinking ordering an under-the-sea cake?" she asked herself. "Abigail will have a fit!"

She opened the door, preparing to return to Lillian's and order a nice, normal cake with roses made out of icing and pearls looping along the edges.

"But Trina will love that under-the-sea cake," she told herself in the rearview mirror.

Lorraine could just imagine the look on her sister's face when she walked into the Drake and saw it.

She closed the door and started the car again.

Her eyes slid shut and she leaned forward, resting her head on the steering wheel as the idling engine purred. What mattered more? Making sure her mother didn't have a stroke over a cake, or her sister's happiness?

In any normal family it wouldn't even be a question, but no one would dare call her family normal. The owners of Hawthorne-Hayes Jewelers? The very pillars of Chicago's elite? Normal?

"Anything but," Lorraine said with a tortured sigh.

Her mother had instilled in her children that to be a Hawthorne-Hayes was to be dignified, distinguished and, above all, the consummate model of decorum. An elegant, sensible cake with delicate, sugared flowers and icing made to look like lace was dignified. It was the kind of cake her mother would approve of. The kind Abigail Hawthorne-Hayes would *demand*.

For that reason alone, Lorraine put the car in Reverse and backed out of the parking space.

To hell with what Abigail wanted. This bridal shower wasn't about her mother; she was doing this for her sister.

Lorraine exited the garage and turned right. As she approached the intersection at Michigan Avenue and East Delaware Place, a thought occurred to her. If she was going to incur her mother's wrath, she might as well make it worth it. She flipped on her right blinker and drove down a block, turned left and then made another left, pulling her car up to the valet at the Drake.

Her mother had insisted on elegance and refinement when it came to the bridal shower, but she could save that for the wedding. As maid of honor, Lorraine was in charge of shower preparations, and she would give her sister something that fit her personality. That cake she'd ordered at Lillian's was just the start.

Lorraine walked up the carpeted steps leading to the landmark hotel's lobby. As she entered, her eyes were instantly drawn to the enormous flower arrangement in the center of the room, sitting just below the signature crystal chandelier. Opulence oozed from every square inch of the place.

Lorraine met with the hotel's special events coordinator. As she described her new vision for Trina's bridal shower, she had a hard time containing her amusement at the way the woman's face transformed from gleeful to completely horrified. The coordinator's penciled-in eyebrows formed perfect peaks as Lorraine explained that she wanted the calla lily centerpieces replaced with seashells and coral on a bed of soft white sand. She wanted the walls draped in flowing light blue silk, mimicking the waves of the ocean.

The woman cleared her throat. "This all sounds lovely, Ms. Hawthorne-Hayes. However, are you sure we shouldn't discuss this with *Mrs.* Hawthorne-Hayes before making such drastic changes?"

"No," Lorraine said. "I'm the one in charge of my sister's wedding shower. I have the last word. I will browse the web for some ideas and email them to you. Feel free to do the same."

Her mother would have a fit, but Lorraine would deal with it. For once, Abigail Hawthorne-Hayes was not getting her way.

Carter leaned back in the chair and crossed his feet on top of his desk. He used a stylus to make notations on the inventory list he kept stored in his electronic tablet. Ever since they were featured at a Chicago Bulls pregame event, Lillian's red velvet cupcakes with dark chocolate and cream cheese frosting, designed in the team's colors of black and red, were flying out the door. Carter needed to increase the order of cupcake holders to keep up with the significant spike in sales.

There was a knock on the door. He looked up to find his cousin Monica. "Carter, were you supposed to have a cake for Maria Salazar ready for today?"

He frowned. "No, that isn't until Thursday."

"Well, she's in the showroom right now to pick up her cake."

Rising from his chair, Carter switched to the app that he used to keep track of his cake orders. He had a cake for an Arabian Nights–themed *quinceañera* scheduled for pick up on Thursday by Maria Salazar.

He turned the screen so Monica could see for herself. "She's not supposed to pick it up until Thursday."

"Well, somebody got their dates crossed. You need to go out there and talk to her."

"I didn't take the order," he said. "It was probably Drake. I think he was working the retail store that morning."

"You're the one listed as the baker. You were specifically requested," she pointed out. Carter didn't miss the smug undertone of his cousin's voice.

The Drayson grandchildren got along well enough, but in jockeying for position in the bakery, Carter definitely had a target on his back. Both their grandparents and his aunt and uncle had taken notice when customers started requesting Carter by name, and so had his cousins.

That wasn't his problem. If the rest of the Drayson clan wanted to stand out, they needed to step up their games.

What *was* his problem was this mix-up with Mrs. Salazar's cake order. It didn't matter who had caused it. As Monica had just pointed out, he was the head baker on the project, which meant he was ultimately responsible for the customer's one hundred percent satisfaction.

Carter entered the showroom, his eyes roaming around for Drake. Of course, his cousin was nowhere to be found. He was probably in one of the back offices playing around on Facebook or Twitter. Somebody needed to remind him that the same social networking he used to tout Lillian's qualities could be used by unhappy customers to eviscerate the company's good name if there were too many mix-ups like the one that had apparently taken place with the Salazar cake.

Carter walked up to the woman who was standing in front of the counter. "Mrs. Salazar, how are you?" he greeted.

"Where is my cake?"

"I don't have you scheduled until Thursday to pick up the cake."

"No, the *quinceañera* is tonight. I was told the cake would be ready by noon." Her elevated voice caused several shoppers to turn their heads.

"Why don't we move over here?" Carter said, gesturing for her to follow him to the rear left side of the showroom, which had been converted into a coffee bar. "Can I offer you something to drink? A latte? Cappuccino?"

"I want my cake," Mrs. Salazar said.

"I found the original order form." Monica came up to them. "It has Thursday marked off, but today's date is written on it."

Great. Carter bit back a curse.

"So I will have no cake for my daughter's *quinceañera?* Is that what you're telling me?"

"Not to worry," Carter said. "Just tell me where it is being held and I'll have your cake delivered by five o'clock."

"Carter," Monica warned in a low tone.

He held a hand up to his cousin, keeping his full attention on Mrs. Salazar. "You'll have the cake you ordered. I will see to it personally," Carter assured her.

The worry lines creasing the woman's forehead lessened, and a cautious smile relaxed the corners of her mouth.

"Thank you," she said. She held up her checkbook. "I still need to pay the balance on the cake."

"No, you don't. It's on us."

"Carter!" Monica sputtered.

"I'm very sorry for the mix-up," Carter said, putting an arm around the woman's shoulder and guiding her to the door. "And tell your daughter happy birthday."

The woman thanked him profusely as she exited the bakery. After she left, he turned and stalked straight to the kitchen, with Monica hot on his heels.

"Do you want to explain to me what just happened there?" she asked him.

Ignoring her, Carter sought out one of the assistant bakers. "Jason, have you baked the cake for the Richardsons' fiftieth wedding anniversary?"

"Yep, it's in the cooler," Jason Parker answered.

"Good. I'm going to have to use it. Can you set it up in my normal work area? And I'm going to need to make spun sugar for the decorations, so can you get me the light corn syrup, too?"

"Would you stop ignoring me?" Monica said. "Now, what happened with Mrs. Salazar's order?"

Carter whirled around. "You know what happened," he said, trying to keep his frustration in check. "Somebody dropped the ball, and now I've got to clean up the mess. Thankfully, the Richardson event isn't until tomorrow night. Their cake is the same size and flavor as the Salazar cake."

"And what about forgiving the balance on her order?"

Carter gritted his teeth. "It's called keeping the customer happy, Monica. I don't know who made the mistake here, but someone had to make it right. Now, can you please get out of my way? I've got a cake for three hundred that I need to construct and replacement cakes that I'll have to stay here for hours baking tonight."

"This should never have happened," she said.

"Damn right, it shouldn't have happened, but it did. Now move out of my way so I can fix it."

Carter tore past her and headed for the cooler, pissed that someone else's incompetence was now on his head.

And would he get any thanks for correcting the situation?

"Not in this lifetime," Carter snorted.

He was so tired of dealing with this crap. He busted his ass in this kitchen, but did he get any thanks for the extra effort he put in?

It was time he faced facts. Nothing he did would ever measure up. He was fighting a losing battle. His cousins would always have a leg up on him.

Carter backed up against the wall of the walk-in cooler and closed his eyes tight.

"Why in the hell am I even doing this?"

Why did he keep coming back for more, like a boxer who kept getting up from the mat after every knockdown, too stupid to leave the ring? It was a question he'd asked himself more than once; he had yet to come up with an answer that made sense.

Chapter 3

"What are you doing? What are you doing?" Lorraine chanted quietly to herself as she walked along Michigan Avenue.

This was a bad idea. She should turn around and go right back to her car. Now. Before she did something she'd regret. Or, even worse, before she made a fool of herself.

She looked up and spotted the ornate gold-leaf lettering etched across one of the huge bay windows of Lillian's. There was still time to turn back. In fact, she could just keep walking forward, round the block and return to the parking garage.

Before she succeeded in talking herself out of doing it, Lorraine wrapped her hand around the brass-plated door handle and pulled. She stepped into the bakery, taking a moment to breathe in the heavenly aromas of cakes, pies, cookies and coffee. She looked around the showroom, with its crystal chandeliers, marble floors and counters and richly decorated cakes, but she didn't spot the one thing she was hoping to catch a glimpse of: Lillian's charismatic cake maker. She wasn't sure whether to feel disappointed or relieved.

Relieved, she decided. Carter Drayson would have seen straight through her flimsy excuse for returning to the bakery so soon.

"Back again?" came a voice over her shoulder. "Can I help you with something else?"

Lorraine turned. It was the same guy who'd greeted her yesterday. Dre? Drake? She wasn't sure of his name; she only knew he was a member of the Drayson family.

"Hello," she said, slipping her hand into her purse to grab the picture she'd brought with her. Then she thought better of it. The picture was the pretense she had planned to use if she'd run into Carter.

"I…I wanted to try a petit four," she said, stumbling over her hastily concocted excuse. "It wasn't until I left the bakery yesterday that I remembered that Lillian's is known for its petit fours."

"They are the best in the city," he said.

Lorraine followed him to the glass display case, with its ornate gold filigree and dozens of square petit fours, lady fingers, delicate French lace cookies, fruit tarts and other delicacies.

"Everything looks so delicious," she said. "I will take two petit fours and one chocolate-dipped short-bread cookie."

As he packaged her purchase in a brown-and-pink-striped bakery box, Lorraine almost asked if Carter was in the back. She stopped herself just in time.

It was pure insanity, her sudden obsession with this man. She was not some fifteen-year-old with a girlhood crush. She was a grown woman who knew all too well the havoc being a starry-eyed, love-struck fool could cause. As of this moment, her preoccupation with Carter Drayson was over and done. As soon as she got her sweets, she would leave this store and not return. She would simply email him the picture of Trina scuba diving on her trip to the Caymans.

Lorraine took the box from Dre or Drake—she no longer cared what his name was—and headed for the exit.

"Lorraine?"

A bolt of awareness coursed down her spine at the sound of Carter's voice. He approached, smelling like sugar and chocolate. And wasn't *that* the definition of irresistible?

"Carter! Hello!" Lorraine knew her overly bright smile must look as fake as the cubic zirconias people tried to pass off as diamonds when they came to her family's jewelry stores.

"Were you leaving?" he asked.

She would have guessed it was pretty obvious. She had her purchases in one hand and the other was wrapped around the door handle.

"Yes, I was," she said. "I came in to try Lillian's petit fours. I realize that I ordered a cake but actually have no idea of the quality of the product."

She grimaced as soon as the words left her mouth. *Tell the man you want to make sure his cake won't suck. Brilliant.*

Lorraine would have given anything for someone to run out from the kitchen and yell "fire." Then she immediately felt like a brat for wishing harm on the bakery simply to extricate herself from a horrifyingly embarrassing situation. This awkward "open mouth, insert foot" feeling was foreign to her.

"Not that I don't think Lillian's cakes are anything but exceptional," she said, trying to atone for her previous gaffe. "The bakery has been touted as one of the best in Chicago for years."

"My apologies for not insisting on a tasting when you came in yesterday. We usually do. It was a hectic morning and I wasn't thinking straight."

"Oh, no, please don't apologize. A tasting isn't necessary. The petit fours are enough."

"If you're sure," Carter said. A subtle smile lifted the corner of his mouth. It was accompanied by a flash of awareness that sparkled in his eyes. "Is that the only reason you stopped in, or is there something else I can do for you? I meant what I said yesterday. You're welcome to come by anytime. For anything."

Lorraine just stood there for a moment, staring at the way his lips formed the words. She jerked to attention and shook her head. He had an amazing knack for annihilating her good sense.

"Actually, I also came to bring you this." Balancing the box of pastries in one hand, she reached into her purse and retrieved the picture of Trina. "This is my sister and her fiancé on a scuba diving trip last summer. I thought it could serve as inspiration when you design the cake."

As Carter took the picture from her, his fingers lightly grazed her palm. The simple touch set off a cataclysmic reaction within her, shooting electric sparks of heat from the top of her head to the tips of her toes, and to all parts in between.

"They make a nice couple," Carter remarked. He motioned for her to follow him to a corner of the bakery, stopping next to a table with brownies packaged in cellophane and tied with curly ribbons. He looked up from the photo and back to her. "I can tell that you two are twins, but you're definitely different."

"Trina's the fun one," Lorraine blurted. Embarrassment washed over her. Okay, just where in the hell was that fire!

"And you're not fun?" Carter asked.

She could feel the blush creeping up her face. "Let's just say I don't scuba dive."

"There are a lot of things besides scuba diving that I'd classify as fun. I'm sure you've got a dangerous side hidden somewhere in there."

Her mother would have fainted at the unladylike snort that slipped out, but Lorraine couldn't help it. "The most dangerous thing I've done in the past five years was ordering that under-the-sea-themed cake instead of something more refined."

She was suddenly appalled at the truth behind her admission. How had she allowed herself to become this person, a caricature of the hollow socialite she'd vowed never to be?

Actually, she knew exactly how it had happened. She could recall with amazing alacrity the precise moment when she'd shed her rebellious streak and vowed to become the perfect daughter. She just tried not to dwell on that one stupid mistake that had changed the course of her life forever.

"If that's the case, we've got some work to do with you," Carter said with a mischievous gleam in his eyes.

Lorraine found that gleam hard to resist. "Such as?" she asked.

"You need to explore your dangerous side. Maybe trade in that stuffy suit for a leather jacket?" He snapped his finger. "I've got it. You should run away with me to Antigua on a scuba diving expedition."

She choked on a laugh.

"No?"

"I don't think so," Lorraine said. "If I were to accompany you to Antigua, who would bake my sister's cake?"

"Hmm, you've got a point. I wouldn't trust something that important to anyone else. I plan to give that cake my undivided attention. I want to make sure it's perfect."

"I appreciate that," Lorraine said, her face warming as she realized that right now *she* had his undivided attention.

She was amazed at how comfortable she felt around him. Ever since "the incident" she had become so wary of men and their motives that she rarely opened herself up to more than a few moments of conversation. And with good reason. Most of the men she met had an agenda, especially after they discovered she was an heiress to the Hawthorne-Hayes jewelry empire.

Would Carter do the same?

Although, after what she'd learned about the Drayson family while searching the web last night, she knew that Carter also came from significant wealth himself. She'd discovered that the Draysons who owned and operated Lillian's were the same Draysons who played a major role in Chicago real estate. In fact, they owned this entire building. Carter would have no reason to be intimidated by her wealth, as some men were. Or, even worse—and what she encountered more frequently— be on the lookout for ways to cash in.

Yet something still stopped her from revealing her full identity. Maybe it was because she *didn't* know how he'd react, and she wanted to keep things the way they were for as long as possible. Just in case he turned out to be like all the others.

Please don't be like all the others.

Carter took her hand in his. "If you won't let me take you to Antigua, would you consider dinner?"

Her shoulders stiffened in surprise. Had he just asked her out on a date?

A customer walked up to the display table, giving her a chance to process Carter's question.

"So?" he continued when they were alone again in their little corner of the bakery.

Lorraine's first instinct was to decline. Years of being cautious made her want to take a step back. After the incident that had happened five years ago, she didn't have much faith in her ability to judge people, especially men.

Yet something told her that things would be different with Carter. She was unsure whether it was her good sense talking or whether the feeling was based on her body's overpowering reaction to him, but she wanted to say yes.

So she did.

"I'd love to," Lorraine answered.

His eyes widened, as if he had thought she would be harder to convince. That smidgen of vulnerability exposed by his shocked expression went a long way in relieving her anxiety. Maybe he wasn't the all-confident player he'd first appeared to be.

And maybe she was just a bit out of her mind. She'd met him less than twenty-four hours ago. What was she doing agreeing to dinner?

But she refused to take it back. It had been so long since she'd allowed herself the simple luxury of sharing a meal with a man she felt a connection to. She *needed* this. If accepting Carter's dinner invitation turned out to be a mistake, she could always leave. She was older now, wiser. She wouldn't allow what happened before to happen a second time.

"Great," Carter said, that note of disbelief she'd seen in his eyes coming through in his voice. "How about tonight? Is eight okay? Where can I pick you up?"

"Eight o'clock is perfect," Lorraine answered, even though her heart was pounding. "But why don't I meet you at the restaurant?"

He was shaking his head, but Lorraine stood her ground. She wasn't ready to step from behind the curtain of anonymity just yet.

"Fine," he relented. "Meet me at Les Nomades at eight."

"Les Nomades?"

"Yes, have you ever been? Their food is amazing."

Yes, she'd been, and she loved it. But Les Nomades was one of Chicago's most expensive restaurants.

"I have," she said. "But it's been years. I'll meet you there tonight."

The grin that spread across his face warranted a new word in the English language: naughty-sexy. Lorraine sensed that her first instinct had been spot-on. Carter Drayson was dangerous…in the absolute best way.

The sounds of glasses tinkling, silverware clanking and muted conversation faded into the background as Carter sat across the table from Lorraine. The understated elegance of his favorite restaurant set the perfect mood for tonight. It felt as if they were the only two people here.

"How is the duck confit?" Carter asked.

"As usual, it is delicious."

"As usual?" His fork stopped in midair. "I thought you said you haven't been here in years."

She looked at him over the rim of her wineglass, a soft blush dusting her cheeks.

"Perhaps it hasn't been quite as long as that," she said, taking a sip of the '03 Bordeaux.

She was an enigma. A beautiful one, but an enigma all the same. He was still trying to figure out his attraction to her. She was so different from the flashy women he usually dated, but he'd be damned if he hadn't thought about her at least a thousand times today.

Maybe it was the mysterious air about her. So often, the women he dated left nothing to the imagination, both physically and personality-wise. Lorraine was like a puzzle, gradually revealing delicate pieces of herself.

Except for one obvious piece.

"So, now that I've convinced you to join me for dinner, what would it take to convince you to tell me your last name?"

Her alluring smile lit up her eyes. "My last name? I didn't know it was such an interesting subject."

"It wasn't until it proved so hard to uncover. You only listed your first name on the cake order form. You paid for it in cash. Why the big mystery, Lorraine? Are you in the witness protection program or something?"

"Perhaps I go by a single name, as Madonna and Beyoncé do."

"So you're secretly a singer?"

She shook her head and, with a laugh, said, "I can't sing a note."

Maybe not, but her laughter was musical. It traveled along his nerve endings, its soothing, melodic effect causing his skin to pebble. Damn, the woman was giving him goose bumps. This kind of stuff did *not* happen to him.

"I do have a last name," she finally said, setting her wineglass on the linen tablecloth. "But it comes with, shall we say, baggage?"

"I know how that is," Carter said with a nod.

She tilted her head to the side, understanding dawning in those sympathetic brown eyes. "Yes, I can see that you do. Being a scion of one of Chicago's most elite families comes with a lot of responsibility, doesn't it? And scrutiny."

"I get my fair share," Carter said. "And anything I do reflects on the bakery. I won't deny that there's pressure there. I've got enough negativity that I have to fight in my family. I don't want to be the one who does something that harms the reputation of Lillian's."

"My goodness." She let out a deep breath. "We're more alike than I first realized."

"Does that mean you really *do* have a last name?" he asked. "Because I know I have one."

"Would you please stop?" She laughed. "Just Lorraine shall do for now."

"Fine, I'll call you Just Lorraine," he teased. "How did you end up with a name like Lorraine, anyway?" Carter grimaced at the callousness of his question. "I'm sorry. That didn't sound as rude in my head."

She laughed again, the sound still musical. "I'm not offended. I know it's old-fashioned. It's a family name," she explained. "My grandmother's."

"I think that name may contribute to this illusion that you're not fun. How about I call you Rainey?"

"My mother would fall away in a dead faint."

"What? You've never had a nickname?"

She shook her head.

"You mean to tell me that when you were five years old and wrote on the walls with crayons, your mother actually called you Lorraine? Not Rainey, or Lainey, or Pumpkin?"

"Pumpkin?" She laughed even harder. "No, it has always been Lorraine. And if Mother was really upset, it was Lorraine Elise."

"Uh-oh, the first and middle name treatment. I've been there. Nearly got myself kicked out of the house a few times."

Her eyes widened. "Your parents threatened to kick you out of the house?"

"Two households," Carter said. "Spent half the time with Dad and the other half with Mom, but I wreaked havoc equally on both."

"I went through a rebellious phase," Lorraine said, poking at the duck confit with her fork. "I discovered a taste for sneaking out. The coup de grâce occurred when I borrowed one of the cars and went joyriding. The police pulled me over in South Bend, Indiana."

Carter let out an overly exaggerated, shocked gasp. "The non-fun twin? No way," he said, grinning at her. "Did that warrant a Lorraine Elise from your mother?"

"Unfortunately not. Instead, Trina and I received one-way tickets to a boarding school in the hinterlands of upstate New York." She pushed the garnish around her plate. "So much for my play for Mother and Father's attention."

The underlying note of sadness in her voice caused something in Carter's chest to squeeze tight. The two of them really *were* more alike than either of them had first thought. How many boneheaded things had he done as a kid so he could stand out from the pack of Drayson grandchildren?

"So, have you officially buried that rebel who used to sneak out and steal cars?" he asked her.

"She's still lurking, but she's much tamer."

"That's too bad," he said. "Sounds as if I could talk her into doing some pretty wild stuff."

"I don't think that would be very difficult. Look how quickly you convinced me to have dinner with you." She glanced at him from across the table, that blush blossoming on her cheeks again. "I'm not usually this easy."

"Well, that's encouraging," he said, settling back in his chair and smiling over the rim of his wineglass as he took another sip.

Carter still wasn't sure just what it was about her that had ensnared him, but he couldn't deny that Lorraine had him in her clutches. Maybe it was that adorable shyness, or her prim and proper speech. More than likely it was that spark of rebelliousness peeking out from underneath the surface. No doubt that hint of naughtiness he'd observed in her eyes appealed to him. He was looking forward to peeling back the many layers of the woman sitting across from him.

The waiter arrived with the single dessert Carter had ordered for the two of them to share.

"Okay," he said, holding out a spoonful of ginger crème brûlée. "I have a confession to make. Even though this really is one of my favorite restaurants in the city, I had an ulterior motive in bringing you here. The head pastry chef was my chief rival back in culinary school," Carter explained. "You sampled my desserts earlier today. I want you to tell me which is better."

Her eyes held a glimmer of mischievous humor. "Are you looking for an honest opinion or an ego stroking?"

"Honest opinion," he said.

She leaned forward slightly and parted her lips. For

several moments all Carter could do was stare at her delicate pink tongue and think about all the ways he could enjoy it. Shaking off the rush of instant lust, he pulled in a deep breath and slid the spoon inside her mouth.

Lorraine closed her eyes and let out a soft moan.

"It's horrible. So bad that I won't subject you to it," she said, reaching for the shallow, oblong dish.

"Nice try." Carter laughed as he scooped up a spoonful of the custard and ate it. "Dammit, it's amazing."

"I'm certain that if you made a crème brûlée it would be as good or better."

He shook his head. "Mine is okay, but it can't compare to this."

"Forgive my table manners, but that looks too delicious." Lorraine reached over and scooped up a helping of the Chantilly cream used to garnish the dessert, and sucked it from her finger. "Mmm…it's glorious," she said.

Carter's chest constricted as every bit of blood in his body headed straight for his groin. He quickly scooped up some of the cream and held his finger out to her.

"Please do that again." His voice held a miserable plea, but he didn't care.

Lorraine hesitated for a moment, uncertainty flashing across her face, but then she obliged. Her eyes never leaving his, she parted her lips and closed them around his finger.

"Mmm," she said. "I was right about you. You're a dangerous man, Carter Drayson."

"Is that good or bad?" he managed to ask, despite the tightness in his throat.

"Probably both."

"How so?"

In a slightly lower, slightly awe-filled whisper, she

said, "You make me want to do things I'd never before considered doing on a first date."

There was no mistaking the look in her eyes. He'd seen it in the eyes of countless other women, but Lorraine looked even hungrier than most. Carter felt light-headed. "Are you ready for the check?"

"Yes," Lorraine quickly answered.

The extremely attentive waitstaff at Les Nomades had their plates cleared in no time, and five minutes later, Carter had taken care of the check. He rounded the table and pulled out her seat, then settled his hand at the small of her back as he guided Lorraine out of the restaurant.

Les Nomades was within walking distance of the bakery, so he'd left his car parked in his usual spot. But Lorraine had driven here. As they waited underneath the awning for the valet to bring her car around, Carter told himself to slow down.

But he couldn't. He had to taste her.

He leaned forward, his heart pounding in anticipation of the way Lorraine's lips would feel against his.

Just then, a flash of lightning streaked across her face. Wait. That wasn't lightning. It was a camera flash.

"Oh, goodness. No." Lorraine held her purse in front of her face.

"Hey, what the hell?" Carter tried to stiff-arm the guy with the camera, but he got in one more shot before taking off.

Lorraine looked up at him with wild, frightened eyes.

"It's okay," Carter said, capturing her forearms and giving them a squeeze.

"No. No, it's not." She shook her head. "I'm sorry, but I have to go."

The valet picked that moment to pull up with her

car. Before Carter could fully comprehend what was happening, she handed the valet a twenty-dollar bill, slipped behind the wheel and was gone.

Chapter 4

Lorraine pulled into her designated parking spot and grimaced when she spotted her brother's car. She loved him, but she had no desire to listen to Stuart and her father lament over inventory or diamond cuts or any other business-speak tonight. She grabbed her clutch from the passenger seat before getting out of the car, then shut the door and leaned against it. Lorraine closed her eyes, sucking in a deep, cleansing breath.

What had she almost done?

She would have slept with Carter Drayson tonight. There was no doubt in her mind. If she'd allowed him to get in the car with her, she would have fallen into bed with a man she'd met a little over twenty-four hours ago. She wasn't so sure they would even have made it to a bed. Lorraine feared she would have demanded he pull over into a dark alley so they could go at it right in the car.

"What's gotten into you?" she said aloud as she pushed away from the car.

She was *not* this type of person anymore—some stupid, impulsive girl who disregarded all common sense because a good-looking man showed her a bit of attention.

She needed to take a step back, away from the spell Carter Drayson had woven around her. Even though everything inside her was telling her that Carter was being true, she just didn't know enough about him to make a sound judgment call. Hadn't she learned anything from her past mistakes?

Another man with a charming smile flashed in front of her eyes, and Lorraine's stomach roiled. She'd tried to eradicate Broderick Collins from her psyche, but, apparently, five years was not long enough to purge such ugliness. She'd been down that road before; she wasn't about to make a return trip.

She boarded the elevator that took her up to her family's penthouse. Lorraine heard the muted, but distinctive voices of her father and her brother as soon as she entered the apartment. She attempted to be as quiet as possible as she slipped past the sitting room where the two of them were having a drink.

"Lorraine, I need to see you," her father said.

Her chin dropped to her chest. She was not up for this tonight. Whatever *this* was.

She turned and walked into the sitting room that served more as an informal office for her father. He had a real office on his and her mother's side of the penthouse, but he usually entertained business associates in this room.

Her father and her brother both sat in leather wingback chairs, holding highball glasses filled with amber-colored liquid. Her father held a sheaf of papers in one of his hands.

Arnold Hawthorne-Hayes was a huge man. Not fat. Never fat. But he had always been larger than life, with broad shoulders and an even broader countenance. Even though she'd lived with him for nearly all of her twenty-five years, Lorraine couldn't say she knew the man all that well. He'd always been too busy building his empire; he didn't have time to bother with something as trivial as being fatherly to his children.

"It's just after ten o'clock," Lorraine said. "I still have two more hours before my curfew." She inwardly cringed. She would gain nothing by intentionally antagonizing her father.

"I don't care what time you come home, Lorraine. What I care about is this." Her father held up the papers. "Why are you trying to get a fellowship?"

She stared at the documents, her mouth falling open in disbelief. "How do you even know about that?"

"Because Warner Mitchell is one of the trustees responsible for making the decision," Stuart piped in. "We were having lunch at the country club today and he wanted to know why my sister would need to apply for an artist fellowship, when the Hawthorne-Hayes Foundation already funds dozens of scholarships. I want to know the same thing."

"It wasn't about the money," Lorraine said. She'd donated five times what the fellowship was worth to the school. This particular fellowship wasn't just a need-based award. It was also talent-based.

"Do you know how embarrassing it was to have Warner ask me that question in front of everyone?" Stuart asked.

"Forgive me, Stuart—I didn't know my art was such an embarrassment."

"I'm tired of this, Lorraine," her father stated. "I allowed you to pursue your art degree when you should have studied business as your brother and sister did, but I refuse to allow you to bring shame on this family's name by soliciting fellowship money."

He ripped the application in half.

Lorraine stared in disbelief at the tattered pages her father tossed onto the glass table between his and Stuart's chair.

"This had nothing to do with the family name. I didn't want the family's name to have any influence over the selection committee."

"You are a Hawthorne-Hayes," her father said. "That name will always have influence." He gave her a pointed look. "Forget the fellowship. This family gives to charity—it doesn't take it."

Lorraine stood in the middle of the room, seething.

She didn't need additional proof of her skill as an artist. Many of her paintings had already garnered much acclaim across the city, but only a select few knew that up-and-coming erotic artist L. Elise and Lorraine Hawthorne-Hayes were one and the same.

She was ready to step from behind the shadows of L. Elise's paintings. Despite the success of her erotic art, a part of her still questioned whether that success had more to do with the subject matter than the artistic style. She wanted to be known for the less provocative, but equally arresting art she created as simply Lorraine.

That fellowship had been a way to prove to herself that her success was not due to the shock factor of her risqué subject matter, but because of her God-given talent. And it would also show her family that her achievements had nothing to do with being a Hawthorne-Hayes.

Her entire life she and her siblings had been accused of using their family's influence to get ahead. Stuart didn't mind; in fact, her brother had no problem throwing around the fact that he was a Hawthorne-Hayes, if it meant he'd get his way.

Despite being a free spirit, Trina had done exactly as expected. When she earned her MBA this fall, she would step right into her role at Hawthorne-Hayes Jewelers, and be the perfect little daughter their father had always hoped she'd become.

How appropriate that Lorraine, his mother's namesake, couldn't stomach the idea.

"May I please be excused?" she asked.

Her father didn't speak, just gave a firm nod.

Lorraine fought back angry tears as she walked to her room. The tornado of emotions rolling inside her made her want to burst out of her skin. There was more to life than just being heir to the Hawthorne-Hayes empire. She needed to *do* something with her life. Create something. She'd been blessed with a talent that she knew was not a fluke. She'd received enough feedback from people who had no idea what her last name was—patrons of Chicago's art scene who had praised the soulful passion of her L. Elise paintings.

Lorraine Hawthorne-Hayes wasn't a jeweler. She wasn't a businesswoman. She wasn't a socialite.

She was an artist.

She needed to find a way to share her true self with the world, to actually *do* something with it.

"Gosh, you are so pathetic," Lorraine said with a sigh as she stepped out of her shoes.

No, she wasn't pathetic. She was just…lost. And confused.

For the past five years, she'd gone to great lengths to present to the world a sophisticated woman who had it all together on the outside, but on the inside she was a complete mess. There was a war waging inside her, and she had no idea which side should win. Her loyalties were divided between what she wanted and what her parents demanded of her, and unfortunately, what should have been an easy choice to make had been complicated by her own stupid mistakes.

She owed her parents everything. Without their help with the nightmare that was Broderick Collins, she would have been publicly humiliated, unable to show her face anywhere. A part of her felt as if she should just fall in line and be the dutiful socialite that her mother and father wanted her to be.

But an even stronger part of her was yearning to allow her creative side to blossom.

Lorraine washed the makeup from her face, put on her nightgown and slipped between the cool sheets on her bed. When she closed her eyes, she saw her father ripping up that document, and the tears she'd tried to stave off started flowing down her cheeks.

That fellowship would have been the validation she'd been seeking, the proof that she was so much more than just her name. This battle between living up to her family's expectations and living the life she just *knew* she was destined to live was exhausting. How would she ever meld the two?

Carter loaded the sheet pan into one of the bakery's industrial-size ovens. Today was a rare day off for him, but he'd decided to come in and give Malik a hand in the kitchen. His original plans had consisted mainly of catching up on a couple of crime dramas he had stored on his DVR, but Carter knew he wouldn't have been able to concentrate on television. For the past twelve hours, all he had been able to think about was how his date with Lorraine had ended.

Having some random photographer snap their picture was strange enough, but why had she run like a scared rabbit? Last night, he had teased her about being in some type of witness protection program, but now Carter was starting to believe there was merit behind his joke. She refused to disclose her last name. She wouldn't allow him to pick her up at her house. And she totally freaked out at having her picture taken. What other explanation was there for the mystery surrounding her?

Carter emptied the remaining batter for Lillian's Lemon-Raspberry Bars into a second sheet pan and slipped it in next to the first one, programming the timer on the oven's computer panel. He carried the dirty bowls, beaters and spatula to the washroom and wiped down his station, and then he went in search of Malik. He found his best friend stretched out on the sofa in the empty office that was used as a break room. He had a newspaper spread out across his lap.

Carter flicked the towel he'd draped over his shoulder at Malik's head, catching him on the ear.

"What the hell?" Malik scrambled to sit up and turned to glare at Carter.

"That's my question," Carter replied. "I come in on my day off to help you and find your lazy ass lounging with the paper? What's up with that?"

"I'm on a break," Malik argued. "Now, why don't you tell me why you've been holding out on me?"

Carter's brows rose in question.

"This." Malik held out the Arts & Entertainment section of the paper. "You've been seeing a Hawthorne-Hayes and didn't bother to rub it in anyone's face? That's not like you."

Carter snatched the paper from him. On the front page of the A&E section, in full color and above the fold, was a picture of him and Lorraine last night in front of Les Nomades. The caption under the picture read Jewelry Heiress Lorraine Hawthorne-Hayes Is Showcasing New Bling.

"When did you start dating her?" Malik asked.

"I didn't… I'm not. I mean…" But he couldn't finish his response. He just stared at the picture, registering the pure shock and horror the photographer had captured in Lorraine's eyes.

"I know you're a Drayson and all, but she's pretty rich even for your blood," Malik added.

"I didn't know who she was," Carter said, still unable to tear his eyes away from the photograph. "I only know her as Lorraine. She never told me her last name. I guess this is why," he said, gesturing to the picture. He folded the paper and tucked it under his arm.

"So, how serious is it?" Malik asked. "You plan on going ring shopping soon? I'll bet Daddy Hawthorne-Hayes would give you a discount."

"Shut up," Carter told him. "I only met her a couple of days ago when she came in to order a cake for her sister's bridal shower."

"You've only known her for a couple of days and already took her to Les Nomades? Damn, maybe you *will* be ring shopping soon." Carter glared at him, but Malik only laughed. "You know I'm just messing with you, man. I had to put up with enough flak from you when things got serious between me and Belinda. I deserve to get some payback."

"Nobody said this thing with Lorraine was serious," Carter countered. "I'm not about to get shackles around my wrists like you."

"Hey, man, don't knock it until you try it. I didn't realize just how empty my life was until Belinda and I got together."

Carter rolled his eyes. "Please spare me the sappy love song lyrics."

"Whatever," Malik said. Then his expression took on a more serious edge, and his voice lowered as he asked, "Now that you're dating, does this mean that other thing you're thinking about is off the table?"

"No." Malik was the only one he'd told about his conversation with the restaurateur in New York. "Tell me you haven't told Belinda about any of this."

"I told you I wouldn't," his best friend said. "Just promise me you'll think this through, Carter. Lillian's needs you. Don't make any rash decisions."

"If I were in the business of making rash decisions, I'd be gone already," Carter pointed out. "I'm weighing all of my options, but when I finally do make a decision, it'll be the one that's best for *me*."

The door swung open and Drake entered the break room. "Hey, what are you two up to?"

When Malik looked over at Carter with a note of inquiry in his eyes, Carter gave his head a subtle shake. He didn't want Drake's opinion on either of the topics he and Malik had just discussed.

"Nothing," Malik said. "What's up?"

"We need to talk about the cookbook," Drake started. "I heard from the publisher earlier today. They're ready to move forward on this ASAP."

"Damn, they're that eager to cut us that fat advance check?" Malik asked.

"More likely they're eager to jump on the bandwagon of the *Brothers Who Bake* blog," Carter said. "Can't say I blame them."

"My entry with the white chocolate, macadamia and pineapple cake bars had over five thousand hits," Malik bragged.

"That's a good recipe. We need to include that one in the book," Drake said, grabbing a pen and steno pad from a side table. "We also need to figure out who will write which portions. It makes sense for Carter to do the entire section on cake baking and decorating, since that's his specialty. Malik, you're the guy who does brownies, cookies and bars."

"Hey, I do more than just that," Malik said with an affronted frown.

"We all do more than just one thing," Drake pointed out. "And we're all going to have some input into everything that goes in the book. But I think for the first pass, we should work with our strengths."

"Have they set a deadline yet?" Carter asked, thinking about his own timetable. He knew he would have to make a decision about the job in New York sooner rather than later, and with the *You Take the Cake* competition coming up, and the mystery that was Lorraine Hawthorne-Hayes now occupying every bit of space in his brain, his mental plate was full.

"Once we sign the book contract, we have six months to get the first draft to them," Drake said. "And that includes detailed recipes and photographs. I think the smartest way to tackle this is to brainstorm the recipes we want to include in the book, and clear an afternoon so we can bake them. We hire a photographer to come in and take all the shots, and it's done."

"Sounds like a plan," Carter said.

"So, we're definitely doing this, right?" Drake asked.

"I'm in," Malik said.

"Hell yeah," Carter added. "With the blog, this book and *You Take the Cake,* Lillian's is about to hit the big time."

He just wondered if he would be around to see it all happen.

Lorraine used the pad of her thumb to fill in the white space on the canvas. She was working with charcoal today. It was a medium she rarely used, but the somber shades of gray matched her melancholy mood.

It never ceased to amaze her how rapidly things could go downhill.

Last night had started out practically perfect. Carter had been the ultimate flirt, but also the consummate gentleman, to the point of almost charming her right out of her panties.

Almost.

Thank goodness she had not succumbed to her body's craving. In the light of day, without the romance of a fancy dinner and Carter Drayson's deadly charm clouding her judgment, Lorraine knew that going home with him last night would have been detrimental to the image she'd cultivated over the past five years, not to mention the delicate trust she'd been able to build with her parents.

For that alone Lorraine was grateful to the photographer who'd snapped those photos last night. But that was all she was grateful for. She resented the complete disregard for her privacy, and with the emergence of additional online social media, it seemed to get worse every year.

She wasn't foolish enough to think she could keep her identity hidden from Carter any longer, and the thought left her heartbroken. She could usually count on at least a few weeks of being able to just be herself before she was forced to don the Hawthorne-Hayes mantle. Carter would treat her differently; men always did once they discovered she was heiress to part of her family's jewelry empire.

"They can keep their empire," she said as she swiped the charcoal across the canvas with violent strokes.

The guilt that followed was immediate and stinging in its intensity.

She had enjoyed the type of life many people dreamed of. She'd attended the best schools, dressed in the best clothes and had visited more than two dozen countries on lavish summer and winter vacations. She'd never wanted for anything…except her parents' attention.

Thanks to Broderick Collins she'd certainly gotten it, in spades. It brought new meaning to that adage "be careful what you wish for."

"Enough with the pity party," Lorraine admonished herself. But as hard as she tried, she could not shake the gloomy cloud that had been hovering over her all day. She felt as if she were drifting, with no real direction, no purpose.

She looked around her studio, her eyes roaming over the paintings of luscious landscapes, architectural landmarks and the Chicago skyline lined up against the walls, stacked two and three deep. What was the point of all this if they just remained in here, for only her eyes to enjoy?

She needed to do something with these paintings. She needed to find some meaning in all of this.

She wondered what Carter would think if she brought him here to show him her work, and then wondered why his opinion would matter at all. There were people she had known her entire life who had no idea she owned this loft in Chicago's more artist-friendly Wicker Park neighborhood, yet she was thinking of bringing a man she'd met only a couple of days ago here?

What was it about him that elicited such a strong reaction within her? Lorraine didn't have to think too hard to come up with an answer. He had a genuineness about him that was in such contrast to the men she had previously dated. She'd had her fill of artificial men who didn't bother to get to know the real her, men who were only interested in what she could do *for* them as a member of the powerful Hawthorne-Hayes family.

Now that Carter knew who she really was, would it change the way he saw her?

"I hope not," she said with a forlorn sigh.

Her cell phone rang.

Lorraine wiped the charcoal from her fingers with a swatch of ragged linen. She reached for the phone, expecting to see Trina's number, or maybe her mother's, but it was a number she didn't recognize.

"Lorraine speaking."

"Hello, Rainey," came a smooth, familiar voice.

Tremors of excited heat skittered across her skin. A part of her had hoped to never hear from him again after the disastrous end to their date, but an even stronger part had desperately prayed that he'd contact her. She had been *waiting* for him to contact her.

"How did you get this number, Carter?"

"From your order form. You didn't leave your last name, but you did leave a contact number."

She leaned against the floor-to-ceiling window in her loft, staring out at the people going about their day. With a deep breath, Lorraine asked, "Is my name still a mystery to you?"

"No," he answered. "I saw the paper."

"And?" she asked, her breath catching in her throat in anticipation of his response.

"And I'm happy you're not part of the witness protection program or a secret agent in the CIA."

Lorraine let out a relieved laugh. Her anxiety melted, and the relaxed contentment she'd experienced the two times she'd been in Carter's presence eased into place.

"I'm sorry for being so secretive, but after last night I'm sure you can see why," she said.

"Is that what life is usually like for you? People constantly snapping pictures of you?"

"I'm not subjected to the Kardashian treatment on a daily basis, but the Hawthorne-Hayes name carries a fair amount of newsworthiness. It's something I've lived with my entire life, but I will never, ever get used to it."

"I guess when you own half of Chicago, it's tough to keep a low profile."

"I do *not* own half of Chicago," she said. Maybe one-third. "And it's my family, not me."

"But you stand to inherit a part of your family's jewelry empire, don't you?"

Disappointment caused her heart to squeeze within her chest. She had hoped Carter wouldn't be like the others, but apparently, he couldn't see past the wealth connected to the Hawthorne-Hayes name, either.

"Does the pressure get to you, too?" he asked.

Lorraine's back stiffened. "What was that?"

"You know, the pressure that comes with trying to live up to the family's expectations. I know what it's like, remember?"

He did. And her heart melted.

This was what made Carter different. He could identify with her in a way very few men ever could. In the past, whenever she tried to convey the problems she faced being a member of her family, she was met with derision. Men thought she was being a whiny brat, that she should thank her lucky stars that she'd been born into privilege. Carter understood that being born into privilege carried its own burdens.

"What pressures are you under?" she asked softly, her fingers clutching the phone.

He was quiet for several moments; then Lorraine heard him sigh.

"We're in the midst of a transition period at Lillian's. All indications point to my grandparents handing the reins of the business to one of us grandkids in the very near future, and everyone is trying to stand out. I'm starting to question whether it's even worth it, you know? A part of me is ready to say to hell with it and just branch out on my own. Make a name for myself that has nothing to do with the Drayson family dynasty."

"Oh, goodness, I *do* know, Carter. I know *exactly* what you are speaking of. The pressure can be overwhelming."

"It was nice to get away from it all last night."

"Yes, it was," she agreed, an unbidden smile tilting up the corners of her mouth.

"If it was so nice, why did you run away like that?" he asked, accusation layering his softly spoken question. "I wasn't ready for our date to end."

"Neither was I," she said. "The photographer just…

I don't know… He caught me off guard. I didn't know what you would think of me after that happened."

"I think that I never got the kiss I was hoping for," Carter answered. "I'd like the chance to try again."

Lorraine pulled in a deep breath. Was this man real, or was he just a pro at talking a really sweet game? A really, *really* sweet game. Ever since Broderick nearly destroyed her, she had gone to such extreme caution when it came to the men she dated. But she had to take that next step again someday, didn't she?

Why not today? Why not with Carter?

"If I asked you out again, would you say yes, Rainey?"

Even his silly nickname made her body warm from the inside out, especially when he said it in that low, sexy tone.

"Why don't you ask?" she encouraged.

His low chuckle traveled seductively up and down her spine. "Lorraine, would you like to go out with me again?"

She pulled her bottom lip between her teeth. "Yes," she answered. "I'd like that very much."

"Can I pick you up from your home like a gentleman this time?"

She hesitated for a second, but now that he knew who she really was, it seemed silly to hide from him. She gave him her address.

"I'll see you tonight," he said. "Make sure you wear comfortable shoes."

"For what reason?"

"Tonight's plans require a lot more walking than last night's. I just want you to be prepared. I'll pick you up at seven."

Before she could ask just what those plans were, he disconnected the call.

She had known the man for two days, and was already going on her second date with him.

"Hussy," she said, and burst out laughing.

Lorraine looked around the studio, unable to staunch the grin that broke out across her face. Nothing had really changed. She still felt as if she was drifting, unsure of what she should do with the rest of her life. But after months—no, years—of discontent, she had finally found one bright spot: Carter Drayson.

Chapter 5

Carter pulled into the parking garage of the high-rise in Chicago's elite Gold Coast neighborhood. He had not been surprised when Lorraine had told him where she lived, but did she have to live in the biggest, ritziest building on the block?

It was ridiculous to feel intimidated; he had enough money in his own right. But when faced with this type of wealth, Carter couldn't help feeling a bit awed.

He approached the doorman and gave him his name. The uniformed man made a call, then moments later asked Carter to follow him to the elevator. The doorman slipped an electronic card into a slot and pressed fifty-seven. Carter watched the numbers climb as the elevator smoothly rose to the top of the building.

"It's the penthouse. Make a left when you exit," the doorman instructed.

Carter walked down the hallway to the only door on

this floor. He smoothed his hands down the front of his lightweight cashmere sweater, then knocked. He waited a few moments before the door opened.

"Good evening. You must be Mr. Drayson," said the middle-aged woman who answered the door. She, too, was dressed in a uniform. A live-in housekeeper? Was Lorraine really rolling like that? Man, and he thought he was something special because he'd bought himself a Porsche.

"I am," Carter answered. "How are you?"

"Frannie, is someone at the door?" Lorraine came into the room and her face lit up. "Hi," she said, a bit shyly.

"Hi," Carter answered, feeling a smile growing on his face. She tended to do that to him.

The housekeeper stood between them, looking pointedly at Lorraine. She cleared her throat.

"Oh. Gosh. Sorry. Carter, this is Francine, our housekeeper. Frannie, this is Carter Drayson. His family owns Lillian's, the bakery."

"I know it well," the woman answered. "Lorraine doesn't know this, but she's been eating your grandmother's pies since she was a little girl. Of course, I passed them off as my own."

"Frannie!" Lorraine gasped, but then she laughed. "Why doesn't that surprise me?"

"It shouldn't," the housekeeper said. "Have a good time tonight. And because your mother isn't here to say it, I will. Don't stay out too late." Then she left them.

"Do your parents live here?" Carter asked.

"Yes," Lorraine answered. "But don't worry, they're never around. It's usually just me, Trina and Frannie." She pointed to a gold-plated clock sitting on a marble table in the foyer. "You're early. I haven't finished getting ready."

Carter's gaze drifted over her tailored cream slacks and shimmering gold sleeveless sweater. The belt, made out of gold hoops, matched the necklace and earrings she wore. The entire ensemble looked as if it came straight from the pages of a high-end magazine…for the forty-and-over crowd.

Yet on Lorraine it looked just right. How she managed to make an outfit his aunt Daisy would wear look so damn sexy was beyond comprehension.

"What else is there to do?" Carter asked her. "You look fabulous. It's perfect for where we're going."

"Thank you," she said, that demure smile pulling at her lips. "But I'm still not done. Let's go into the living area. I'll fix you a drink."

"I could use a bottle of water," Carter said, following her farther into the penthouse apartment.

Living *area* was definitely the correct word to describe where Carter found himself standing moments later. The space was too vast to be called a simple "room." There were several seating areas with love seats, chairs and low tables set up throughout the space. Marble columns separated the room into quadrants.

The fact that Lorraine lived with her parents had caught him off guard. The lack of privacy would drive him insane. But in a place this size, maybe privacy wasn't an issue. He could get lost just in the living room. Living *area,* he reminded himself.

Yet it was still a bit unnerving that she still lived at home.

"What about your brother?" Carter asked. "Does he live here, too?"

"No, Stuart moved out after he finished college. I've

been telling myself that I will move out eventually. It just hasn't happened yet."

Why not? he wanted to ask. His skin crawled at just the thought of still living with his mom or dad. Instead, Carter said in a teasing tone, "Well, when you have a live-in housekeeper to cook for you, why would you?"

"Now that I know Lillian's has been baking my family's desserts, I'm starting to suspect that most of the meals must come from local restaurants." She gestured to one of the sofas. "Have a seat."

The smooth, comfortable leather enveloped him as soon as he sat. Carter's gaze roamed around the room, taking in the sheer opulence of this place. Everything was done in various shades of white, cream and taupe. From the furniture, to the drapery framing the fourteen-foot windows, to the marble-topped pedestal tables.

His eyes fell on a painting illuminated by the warm glow of a recessed light high above. Carter hopped from the sofa and went over to the wall.

"Your drink," Lorraine said, coming up behind him and handing him a long cylindrical water bottle.

Carter pointed to the painting. "This is a Duchamp."

She blinked several times, as if she was surprised he could spot a painting by the French artist. "Yes," she said. "He's one of my favorites."

"You have an original Marcel Duchamp hanging on the wall." He shook his head. "I knew this place would be something else, Lorraine, but damn."

"Please, do not make a big deal of it, Carter. I know how this must seem over the top to some people, but to me, this is home. It has always been just my home."

"I get it," he said.

"I know you do. It's one of the things I like most about you."

His brows peaked. "Hmm...*one* of the things you like about me? That sounds promising. What are some of the others?"

"I'm not telling you." She laughed. "I think your ego is healthy enough without extra stroking from me."

"Oh, come on. Just one more. Please?" Carter asked with a pleading look that usually led to him getting his way.

"Those puppy dog eyes won't work on me," Lorraine said.

"Are you sure?" he asked, moving a bit closer to her.

She looked up at him. Her big brown eyes sparkled with more than just laughter. There was something else there: heat.

"Fine," she said. She motioned for him to lean over. "I like the way you wear an apron," she whispered in his ear.

Desire shot down Carter's spine at the feel of her warm breath on his skin and the seductive lilt to her voice. When he looked at her, a teasing smile spread across her face.

"Are you ready?" Lorraine asked him.

"For what exactly?" was Carter's reply.

That grin turned coy as she said, "Give me a few minutes more, and then we can leave."

Carter spent the next five minutes observing the other pieces of art in the room. It looked more like a museum than a home, but that was to be expected. He certainly wouldn't find crocheted afghans draped across the sofas in a place like this.

A moment later, he spotted Lorraine walking up the hallway where she'd disappeared earlier. Carter followed her out of the penthouse and into the garage where his car was parked.

"Well, you certainly lived up to my expectations," Lorraine said as he opened the passenger door for her. "I figured you to be the flashy-car type."

"Uh-oh. Do you think less of me now?"

"I didn't say it was a bad thing. It's just an observation," she said, slipping into the car.

Carter rounded the back and got behind the wheel. He started the engine, its gentle purr rumbling softly.

"I've always been a car junkie," Carter explained as he pulled onto North Lake Shore Drive. "I used to have pictures of classic Porsches tacked to my bedroom wall at my mom's house. I crossed an item off my bucket list when I bought this car for my birthday."

"I like it," she said in her prim and proper voice. "It fits you."

"How so?" The fact that he knew so little about her made Carter hyperaware of anything she could read into his personality.

"For one thing, it's a car with personality, and I'm sure it's fast. I can picture you burning rubber along a country road, testing the horsepower."

They were at a stoplight. He revved the engine, just because.

Lorraine laughed. "It's also a very fine-looking automobile."

"Fine-looking, huh? If I'm not mistaken, I'd say that you're flirting with me."

Carter glanced over and caught the reddish hue blossoming on her cheeks. Making her blush was terribly easy, and way more enjoyable than Carter could possibly have imagined.

He also noticed that she'd checked the rearview mirror three times already.

"You think we're being followed?" he asked her.

"Excuse me?" She turned to him, then laughed softly. "I'm still a bit on edge about what happened last night. I'd rather not deal with any paparazzi again this week."

"I have to warn you," he hedged. "There will be media where we're going tonight, but hopefully there will be too much other stuff grabbing their attention than who my date is."

"Where are we going?" Lorraine asked. Carter turned onto North Cannon Drive and pointed straight ahead. "Lincoln Park Zoo? Is the zoo open this time of evening?"

"There's an event to benefit Comer Children's Hospital being held here tonight," he answered. "Lillian's donated the desserts, including four specialty cakes. I deployed a team of six to man the event, but I want to make sure everything is going according to plan. Are you okay with this?" he asked her.

She turned to him. "Of course."

"Are you sure?" Carter asked, finding her swift acquiescence unconvincing. "You understand that this means we're having hot dogs from the concession stand for dinner, don't you?"

Her blithe laughter resonated around the car. "Carter, this is perfect. I mean it," she stressed. "As long as we don't have a repeat of what happened last night cutting our date short, it is perfect."

Perfect. That was what Carter was beginning to think about her.

As they meandered among the crowd, Lorraine couldn't help being charmed by the sights and sounds around her. Even though she lived only a couple of miles away, she had not visited this zoo since she was a little girl, back before she and Trina had been carted off to boarding school in upstate New York. She marveled at the improvements that had been made to the landmark zoo, one of the country's oldest.

"Do you know what that structure is over there?" she asked Carter, pointing to an arched building in the distance.

"Amazing, isn't it? That's the South Pond Pavilion. We'll wind up there eventually. It's where they've set up the cakes."

They forayed farther into the zoo, stopping at various booths that had been set up along the numerous walkways. Carter was continually waylaid by event-goers who had already seen the cakes donated by Lillian's and wanted to remark on their magnificence. He introduced Lorraine to everyone who greeted them, but she'd met a number of the patrons before. Many were members of various boards her father sat on, or politicians who had been on the Chicago social scene for years.

Carter spoke to them all with admirable aplomb and grace, from the highest dignitaries to the average joes. He had a way about him that seemed to put people at ease. But it was the way Carter interacted with the children that had been brought in from the hospital that had a lump forming in Lorraine's throat.

"I know hospital food isn't always the best," he announced to the small crowd gathered around him. "So I brought something extra special just for you guys and girls. Because all of you are extra special."

Carter signaled to one of the workers wearing a pink-and-brown Lillian's T-shirt. The girl brought over a covered tray, and the children gathered even closer around him. Carter lifted the lid to reveal elaborate cupcakes, decorated with zebra stripes, leopard spots and other animal prints. There were even some made to look like sea turtles. The children squealed in delight as Carter handed out the cupcakes.

He dropped to his haunches and wiggled the long braid of a little girl in a wheelchair, who had a trachea tube extending from her neck. The little girl's green eyes lit up as Carter presented her with a cupcake covered with bright pink icing and a plastic flamingo standing proudly in the center.

Lorraine did her best to hold in her emotions, but when she lifted her eyes and spotted a woman she assumed to be the child's mother looking on with tears flowing down her cheeks, Lorraine's own waterworks started their cascade.

How difficult must life be when something as simple as a cupcake could bring so much joy. The notion tugged unmercifully at her heart.

She was suddenly overwhelmed with shame for lamenting over her own problems. She had nothing to complain about. She had her health, her family, a roof over her head and enough money to keep her free from financial worry for the rest of her life. She even had a man with a genuinely good heart interested in her. She was blessed.

She could not fathom the trials these children and their families faced, the pain they had endured. She wished she could do something to lessen their burdens, or at least put the kind of smiles on their faces that Carter and his cupcakes had elicited.

The woman whom Carter had introduced as the coordinator of the event appeared, accompanied by a clown, complete with a bright red nose. The children were all corralled, and the clown began performing a magic show, extracting oohs and aahs from his enraptured audience.

"That was very sweet of you," Lorraine told Carter as they stood a few feet away, watching the clown juggle a collection of colorful rings. "Did you see their faces when you unveiled those cupcakes?"

Carter shrugged. "The kids can get lost in events like this. It's for their hospital, but everything is usually catered to the donors. The kids should feel like the guests of honor."

Lorraine stared at him, warmth settling into her bones. "You're a very thoughtful man, Carter."

"I like giving back," he said. "Especially to kids who don't fit in. I kind of know how they feel."

"You do?"

"I don't know what it feels like to be stuck in the hospital for months, but sticking out like a sore thumb? Yeah, I know how that feels."

Lorraine suspected her skepticism showed on her face, but she couldn't help it. In what universe would he not fit in anywhere he found himself? Taking in the man standing before her, with his gorgeous brown eyes, close-cut, naturally wavy hair, solid, athletic build and seemingly natural ability to converse with anyone and make them feel at ease, she could not imagine Carter ever feeling as if he were on the outside looking in.

Just as she was about to question him, another of the event coordinators came up to them, shaking Carter's hand and thanking him enthusiastically for the show-stopping cakes provided by Lillian's.

"I wish I could see the amazing cakes everyone keeps talking about," Lorraine said when the woman walked away.

"You will, but we've got something else to do first."

She gave him a wary look, not sure she trusted that mischievous glint in his eyes. Carter led her to the amusement park area and purchased two tickets for the carousel. She had not been on a carousel since she was five years old.

"I'll bet you weren't picturing this when you were getting ready for our date tonight, were you?" he asked, holding her hand as she climbed aboard an acrylic horse.

"I'm relieved I opted for pants instead of a dress." Lorraine laughed.

They rode the carousel three times in a row. By the time they were done, Lorraine was dizzy, though she couldn't be sure if it was from spinning in a circle for ten minutes, or laughing at Carter. His ability to make fun of himself was as charming as anything she'd ever encountered.

"Are you ready to see the cakes?" Carter asked as he helped her down from the carousel.

"Yes. Finally."

"Let's go over to the South Pond Pavilion," Carter suggested.

On their way to the arched pavilion where the cakes were on display, they strolled along the Nature Boardwalk, yet another feature that had not been installed the last time Lorraine had visited the zoo. It boasted an array of plant life, birds, insects and other residents of an ecosystem you would never expect to find in the heart of a thriving metropolis such as Chicago.

As anxious as she was to see the cakes, Lorraine had to stop when they came upon a spray of irises. She stooped down and brought a bloom to her nose.

"Heavenly," she said, breathing in the scent. She looked over her shoulder at Carter. "Most people prefer roses, but I just adore irises. They don't get nearly enough credit for their beauty."

They continued on to the South Pond Pavilion. The

wooden structure was a mark of ingenious architectural design. The artist in her could fully appreciate the creativity that went into molding the strong, smooth lines of the wood. It was simply breathtaking.

Lorraine gasped as they came upon the cakes from Lillian's, which were all prominently displayed.

"Carter, these are…" She turned to him. "Unbelievable."

The gorilla had the signature flat face and piercing eyes. The giraffe warranted attention for its sheer size, standing at least five feet, with its face pointing regally in the air.

"Is everything edible?" she asked.

"For the most part," Carter answered. "There's some internal hardware used as reinforcement, but the majority of what you see here is cake and frosting."

"Phenomenal," Lorraine breathed as she rounded the Bengal tiger cake. The stripes and whiskers seemed so real it was a bit frightening.

She pointed to the bird with elaborately colored feathers. "That isn't a peacock, is it?"

"It's a Nicobar pigeon. The zoo is known for the colony that resides here. It's one of the few places you can find them in the United States."

"Fascinating," Lorraine said as she continued to study the cakes. The detail was absolutely outstanding, the animals so lifelike.

"So you approve?" Carter asked.

She whipped her head around. "Is that a serious question? Of course I approve. They are works of art, Carter. Each and every one of them. How long did it take you?"

"It took a team of six of us nearly three days to make these. It was not easy, but it was worth it." He gestured around. "Based on the crowd here, the hospital will pull in a nice sum of money tonight."

Lorraine was about to ask him about the whiskers on the tiger when she let out a yelp. "I do believe that tiger's eyes just moved."

Carter laughed. "Yeah, we incorporated animatronics into it. These days, a fancy cake isn't good enough. You've got to figure out ways to up the ante."

"After seeing these, I cannot wait to see Trina's cake."

"It will be just as spectacular, if not more," Carter promised.

He was so close she could feel the heat coming from his body. Lorraine was almost afraid to believe he could really be as sweet, and funny, and charismatic as he appeared. He was just a sweet talker doing what sweet talkers did, wasn't he?

But what if he wasn't? What if this man, who made her laugh, yet made her blood boil with hot need, was really what he appeared to be? Could she even dare to hope?

"Do you want to take a walk?" Carter asked. "The zoo is magical at night."

Lorraine nodded and placed her palm in his outstretched hand. They ambled along a walkway, moving farther and farther away from the music, laughter and noise. Carter was right: this was magical, with Chicago's distinct skyline stretched out ahead of them and the aroma of fragrant flowers imbuing the air. It was more than just magical; it was heavenly. The entire night had been heavenly.

It occurred to Lorraine that she hadn't thought once about the argument she'd had with her father over the fellowship grant, which had taken up much of her mental energy today. Being with Carter had pushed all of that unpleasantness out of her mind.

Lorraine tucked herself more securely against his side. "I have a question for you," she said. "If it's too personal, please just tell me so."

"Shoot."

"Back there, you said that you knew how those kids felt to not fit in. What did you mean by that?"

"Just what I said," Carter answered. "My last name may be Drayson, but I've never felt as if I was truly one of them. Not the way my cousins are."

"But you *are,*" she said, not understanding. "You're just as much a Drayson as your cousins."

"Biologically, yes, but I didn't have the same experiences they had growing up. I didn't live on the Drayson Estate in Glenville Heights. I visited on some weekends, and most holidays, but I went back and forth between my mom and dad a lot. The rest of my cousins spent their entire childhoods there."

"Do you get treated differently?" Lorraine asked.

He was quiet for several moments before expelling a soft sigh. "This may sound stupid, but I'm not sure." He glanced down at her. "I question it all the time. Am I really being treated like an outsider, or am I reading into things? You know what I mean?" She felt his deep chuckle. "Probably not."

"Actually, I think I do," Lorraine said. He gave her a skeptical look. "I know what you're thinking. I live in a ritzy penthouse and wear designer clothing. I have it made." She swallowed deeply. "Well, appearances can be deceiving, Carter."

He stopped and turned to face her.

"I would never think that anyone's life was all roses simply because they have money," he said. "I may not be rolling in it to the extent that you are, but I know money doesn't buy happiness. I am confused as to why *you* would feel like an outsider, though."

"Perhaps *outsider* is the wrong word. Some may classify it as middle-child syndrome, even though I'm the middle child by only seven minutes. My brother is the golden boy, who could never do anything wrong. Trina has always been seen as the free spirit. My parents tried to contain her, but if you ever met my sister, you would see that their efforts were futile."

"So where does that leave you?" Carter asked.

She paused, measuring her response before she answered, "I was the one who tried to be perfect and often failed miserably."

"I find that hard to believe," he said.

Lorraine snorted an indelicate laugh. "Perhaps you and Arnold Hawthorne-Hayes should meet for drinks and conversation. He could tell you the myriad ways his mother's namesake has disappointed him."

Carter hooked his finger underneath her chin and lifted her head until his eyes met hers. "He must have the most impossible standards on the planet. I cannot imagine you being a disappointment to anyone, Rainey."

Her mouth tipped up in a grin. "He would not approve of that nickname."

Carter's eyes sparkled with laughter. "Then I should probably use it more often."

Cradling her head, he leaned in and met her lips in a slow, gentle kiss that was nothing like Lorraine had expected. Given his personality, she had braced herself for a savage plundering, but Carter surprised her with his tenderness.

She leaned into him, pressing her body flush against his. The heat radiating from every part of him scorched her being, lighting a fire that radiated throughout her bloodstream. A soft mewl escaped her throat as Carter's hand traveled down her spine, stopping at the small of her back. He cradled her waist, and pulled her even tighter against him.

His tongue traced along the seam of her lips, urging them to part, but when they did he didn't plunge inside. Instead, his assault was just as devastatingly tender, which did more to melt her heart than any fiery kiss ever could. His tongue delved in and out of her mouth, gentle, yet insistent, eliciting a moan that tore from her chest.

Carter emitted a groan of displeasure as he reluctantly ended the kiss, but he didn't release her. He continued to cradle her in his arms, the streetlamp casting a soft glow across his face, illuminating the hunger in his eyes.

Gazing up at him, Lorraine whispered, "What is it about you, Carter Drayson?"

That wicked grin returned. "I thought it was the way I looked in an apron."

An instant blush heated her cheeks as she remembered her seductively whispered words from earlier. "You do wear an apron better than any man I know." She shook her head. "But there has to be something else to explain why I'm falling so hard for you, so fast. It is so uncharacteristic of me."

"I know what you mean," he said. "This is new for me, too."

Casting a look of disbelief his way, Lorraine couldn't help the skepticism that colored her voice. "I don't know if I can believe that about you."

"I'm not saying that I'm a hermit who doesn't get out and enjoy himself, but it's never this intense. Or this quick. Do you realize we've known each other less than seventy-two hours? Sometimes it takes me longer than that to pick out my clothes for the weekend."

An unladylike crack of laughter flew out of her mouth before she could stop it. Lorraine shook her head. "I'm trying to decide if you're real, Carter."

"Hey, you're the one who didn't have a last name until today."

"It's just that you seem to have come into my life at just the right time." She looked up at him. "I really needed someone right now."

"Why? What's going on?" He ran a finger down her cheek. The concern in his voice made her throat tighten with emotion.

"I've…I've been feeling a bit…I don't know…stuck. It seems as if everyone else is moving forward with their lives and I'm being left behind."

"Who is everyone?" he asked.

"Since the beginning of the year, five of my friends have either become engaged or gotten married."

"So you're looking to get married?"

Lorraine didn't miss the thread of wary caution in his voice.

"No!" she said quickly. "My goodness, I'm not on the hunt for a husband, Carter. That isn't what I meant." She linked her arms around him and leaned her head against his chest. "You're going to think I'm a horrible person when I tell you this."

"What is it?" he asked, rubbing his palm up and down her back.

"I'm jealous of my sister." Lorraine cringed at the words. "I know it's incredibly selfish of me. Trina has never been happier, and I truly am happy for her. But it has always been the two of us. Now that she's leaving, I just feel…stuck, as if I'm just going through the motions."

She straightened her shoulders and pulled in a deep breath. "Goodness, listen to me. I can only imagine what you must be thinking."

"What do *you* think I'm thinking?" Carter asked.

"The little millionaire heiress is feeling stuck. Poor, unfortunate thing."

"Wrong," Carter said. "I think what you're feeling is completely understandable." He captured her chin between his fingers and she lifted her eyes to meet his. "But it doesn't have to be this way. You can change if you want to."

She shook her head. "You don't understand, Carter. There's more to my life than just what *I* want."

"Like what?"

"Well, the fact that I have responsibilities to my family, for starters. Even though I never asked for them, those responsibilities are still there. As a Hawthorne-Hayes, I'm expected to commit myself to charities and other society functions. Don't mistake my objections. I love my charity work. I'm grateful to be in a position to help so many other people, but most of the time it doesn't feel as if I'm doing enough. There has to be more to life than sitting on charity boards."

"You only have this one life, Lorraine. You can't live it for anyone but you. It doesn't matter what your mother or your father thinks. It doesn't matter what your friends or society thinks." He tapped the shallow space between her breasts. "The only thing that matters is what's in here. Nothing else."

"I wish it were that easy," she said with a sigh.

He captured her chin between his fingers. "It's only

as hard as you make it. When you're ready to take that next step, it'll be the easiest decision you'll ever make."

Lorraine stared into his eyes, once again amazed at how quickly this man had burrowed himself into her world. That ever-present air of caution reared its head again, but Lorraine tamped it down. She wasn't the same person she was when Broderick had weaved his spell around her. She knew better this time around.

Lorraine wrapped her arms more securely around Carter's waist and held on tight. She felt his deep chuckle rumble softly against her ear. She looked up from where she'd lain against his chest.

"What's so amusing?" she asked.

"I was just thinking that I need to take my own advice," he said.

She eyed him curiously, but before she could question him further, Carter leaned forward and captured her lips in another soul-stirring kiss.

Carter became more light-headed with each floor the elevator ascended as they rode it to the penthouse in Lorraine's building, and the feeling had nothing to do with altitude. His body was on fire. After one simple kiss. Well, that wasn't entirely true. There had been nothing simple about that kiss. That kiss had rocked his damn world.

He looked over at Lorraine, standing next to him in the elevator in her stylish slacks and sweater. She looked more like a schoolteacher than a seductive enchantress, but she'd sure as hell cast a spell on him. There was no other way to account for the way his body craved her.

She was such a contrast. The way she'd smiled like a little girl while on the carousel, completely uninhibited, compared with how she'd lit his body on fire with that kiss. She was so much more than what her outer appearance suggested. When he'd first caught sight of her that morning at the bakery, he'd immediately pegged her as a pampered princess, but there was substance hidden beneath the surface. Each hour he was with her, he learned something new. And each new thing made him more and more attracted to her.

The elevator arrived at her floor. As they walked down the carpeted hallway, the blood pounded in his ears.

Lorraine pulled out a key. "Would you like to come in?"

Carter glanced quickly at the door, unsure of what they would find on the other side.

"They're not at home," she said.

His eyes flashed to hers.

"My parents flew to their house in Arizona. Mother has a standing appointment at a wellness spa in Scottsdale once a month. They won't be back for several days."

"So." Carter took a moment to collect his breath. "So no one's home?"

She shook her head. "Trina is spending the night at her fiancé's. Frannie is likely here, but she goes to bed early, and her room is on the east side of the apartment. It's on the opposite side of the building."

"Damn. How big is this place?"

"Big enough that we wouldn't be disturbed," she said, pulling him into the darkened apartment. They walked to the room where he'd been earlier today, and stood before the wall of floor-to-ceiling windows. The view was unlike anything Carter had ever seen. The lights of Navy Pier and downtown Chicago glittered across Lake Michigan, like something you'd find on a postcard.

"That's a pretty amazing view," he said.

She caught his hand and pulled until he faced her. "That isn't the view I want you to concentrate on, Carter."

Lorraine pulled him close and crushed her lips to his, practically inhaling him.

Whoa. What had happened to the sweet, shy woman of just a few minutes ago?

He wasn't questioning it a second longer. Carter followed her lead, snaking his hands down and fitting his palms onto her backside. He pulled her more firmly against him and delved into her mouth with practiced skill. They stood before the window, tasting and exploring, learning each other. And he liked what he'd learned so far.

Lorraine ran her hands up his chest, then wrapped them around his neck. Her soft murmur of pleasure traveled down his spine like a waterfall, causing all manner of electric sparks to shoot across his skin.

Carter fitted her more firmly to his hardening body, his mind picturing her supine, reclining on one of the leather sofas as he peeled the clothes off her.

But that was not what this was about. Not yet.

For some reason, Carter suddenly felt the need to slow things down. The thought shocked the hell out of him. Usually, he approached women with the sole purpose of landing in the situation he now found himself in, hard as a rock with his hands full of a nice, firm ass.

But his normal mode of operation didn't fit when it came to Lorraine. Carter still hadn't figured out what made her so different, but he knew he'd have a good time discovering it.

Reluctantly, he pulled away.

She looked up at him, more than a little dazed and confused. "Is there something wrong?"

He shook his head.

"Then why…?"

"Because you're worth waiting for," he answered.

"But there's no need to wait, Carter."

"Yes, there is. Not much longer," he said, placing a kiss on her forehead. "But we should. I don't want you rushing into this only to regret it later."

She looked crestfallen, making it even harder for him to go along with what his conscience demanded.

"Well, can you join me for a while in the living area?" she asked, tugging him toward the sofa. But Carter knew that was a dangerous proposition. The longer he stayed here, the more likely he would strip the clothes from her body and taste for himself just how sweet she was.

"I'll call you tomorrow," he said. He kissed her again, this time on the lips. "I promise."

And with that Carter let himself out of the penthouse, cursing his sudden spark of gallantry.

Chapter 6

Lorraine spotted Carter as soon as she walked through the doors of Lillian's. He looked up from behind the register where he was ringing up the purchases of a group of women. She swallowed several deep breaths as she waited for him to finish, hoping her nervousness didn't show on her face.

Over the past week and a half, he'd called her at least a dozen times, had texted her at least a thousand times and had taken her out to dinner every night except Sunday, when he'd had dinner with his mother. It had been like a dream, having someone lavish so much attention on her without asking for anything in return. Even though she was desperately ready to give him something very specific in return.

But not today. In fact, today, she had been hoping she wouldn't have to see him at all.

As soon as he was done with his customers, Carter

came from behind the counter and greeted her. "Hey there, beautiful," he said, giving her a quick kiss.

"Carter," Lorraine admonished, looking around the bakery to make sure no one had witnessed his very public display of affection.

"What? They all know what's going on now that our picture was plastered across the newspaper."

"I know it isn't a secret," Lorraine said. He tilted his head to the side and gave her an exaggeratedly forlorn look. "Oh, fine." She stood on her tiptoes and placed a light peck on his lips. "Are you happy now?"

He wiggled his flattened hand. "Marginally satisfied."

"Well, that will have to suffice for now," she said.

"I guess it'll hold me until I see you tonight. What are you doing here, anyway? Shouldn't you be doing last-minute bridal shower stuff?"

"I am," she said. "I'm here to pick up Trina's cake."

"You didn't have to come here. The cake is being delivered. In fact, I'm delivering it personally."

"No!" she shouted much too forcefully.

Carter's head snapped back, his brow furrowing. "Why not?"

"I'm already here and the Drake is only a few blocks away." She gestured toward the large display window. "Bradford, our driver, is outside, ready to do the heavy lifting."

"The cake has to be delivered by people who know what they're doing," Carter said. "Actually, I just had it loaded into one of the delivery vans. It'll be at the hotel in the next ten minutes. You want to meet me there?"

Anxiety tightened her chest, but what could she do, tell him that she didn't want him anywhere around the Drake Hotel today?

"If you insist," she said with forced brightness. "I will meet you there."

A few minutes later, Lorraine was rushing into the tearoom at the Drake, where the finishing touches were being put on the underwater fantasy she and the coordinator had created for Trina's bridal shower.

The woman walked up to her, a cagey smile on her lips.

"Hello, Ms. Hawthorne-Hayes. What do you think?"

"It's breathtaking," Lorraine answered. "Everything I had hoped it would be."

"*Mrs*. Hawthorne-Hayes isn't as thrilled, but I think she's warming up to it."

"Please, do not allow her reaction to bother you," Lorraine said. "My sister is going to adore it, and that's all that matters."

"Lorraine."

She turned to find her mother striding purposefully across the room.

"Yes?" Lorraine answered, ready for a confrontation.

"This theme is not what we discussed for your sister's shower. You planned this from the very beginning, didn't you?"

"That's not exactly true," Lorraine said. "I didn't plan it from the beginning, only after I ordered the cake. And you have to admit that everything is gorgeous, Mother. Trina is going to love it."

Her mother's proud jaw twitched. "I suppose she will." She gave Lorraine a severe look. "But I do not appreciate being kept in the dark. You should have discussed your plans with me."

"You were so busy with all of your other interests. I was tasked with organizing the shower. I didn't feel the need to bother you."

Lorraine turned at the sound of bustling. Seconds later, Carter and one of the other workers from Lillian's came in carrying the most beautiful cake she had ever laid her eyes upon. The cake was everything Carter had promised and more. There were three round cakes in decreasing size stacked upon each other, with what appeared to be hundreds of intricately crafted seashells, sea horses, starfish and other ocean creatures strategically placed on the smooth light blue fondant.

Carter turned to her. "So, is this what you had in mind?"

Before she could stop herself, Lorraine wrapped her arms around him. "Oh, my goodness, Carter, it's perfect."

"I'm happy you like it," he said, pressing a kiss to her temple.

"I must say, the cake is stunning," came her mother's deceptively smooth voice.

Lorraine's spine stiffened at the icy pronouncement. She quickly disengaged from Carter's hold, and took a few steps back.

Carter turned to Abigail and held out his hand. "Hello, I'm Carter, one of the head bakers at Lillian's."

Abigail ignored his outstretched hand. Her eyes embarked on a slow perusal, from the top of his head to his feet, and back. It was clear by the set of her jaw that she found him lacking.

"Thank you for delivering the cake," Abigail said. "Now, if you don't mind, we still have much to do before the start of the bridal shower."

Lorraine was mortified by her mother's dismissal.

Carter's hand dropped, along with his smile. He looked to Lorraine, as if waiting for her to say something more, but what was she supposed to do? Her mother reacted just as Lorraine knew she would, which was why she had not wanted Carter to be the one to deliver the cake in the first place. She wasn't ready to explain him to her parents, and vice versa.

But one look at the injured expression on his face, and Lorraine knew she had to say something.

"Carter, I am so sorry about that," she apologized, taking his hand.

"Lorraine Elise," her mother snapped. Lorraine dropped his hand as if it were a hot iron. "I need you over here right now."

The look in Carter's eyes was one she would never forget. It was filled with hurt, accusation and, worst of all, disappointment.

"Carter," she said with an apologetic plea.

He shook his head. "Don't worry about it."

"You don't understand," she implored.

"Lorraine," her mother called again.

"I understand perfectly," he said. "Enjoy the bridal shower." Then he turned and walked out of the tearoom.

Lorraine fought the overwhelming urge to abandon the shower preparations and race after him. She knew she couldn't leave, but she also didn't want Carter to walk away thinking that she had been ashamed to introduce him to her mother, when, in fact, it was the exact opposite. No one deserved the likes of Abigail Hawthorne-Hayes.

She closed her eyes for a moment, pulling in several deep, cleansing breaths. They did nothing to abate the frustration welling up inside her, but Lorraine was at a loss as to what to do. She'd given her mother good reason to be critical of her choices when it came to men.

Her father might have written the check, but it was her mother who had brokered the deal with Broderick

Collins five years ago, saving their entire family from
the humiliation Lorraine had nearly caused. Of course
Abigail would proceed with caution; she had all but
told Lorraine to her face that she had zero faith in her
judgment.

How could she explain to her mother that Carter was
different?

How did she *know* that Carter was different, especially after knowing him for such a short period of time?

"He is," Lorraine said aloud to herself. She recalled
the way he had so selflessly given of himself at the Children's Hospital Gala at Lincoln Park Zoo. Carter was
sweet, generous, attentive—everything she could ever
want. It scared her to no end to realize she was falling
for him so quickly, but it also felt *right*. It was time she
started trusting her own instincts again.

Once the shower was over, she would go to Carter
and explain her mother's behavior. Although, Lorraine
wasn't entirely sure what was behind it herself. Had her
mother been looking out for her daughter's reputation, or
her own? With Abigail, one never knew the real motive.

As the shower festivities got into full swing, Lorraine
tried to join in on the fun, but her heart was still heavy
over the way Carter had looked at her as he'd left the
hotel earlier today. Every time Lorraine even glanced
in her mother's direction, she wanted to lash out at her.

Her eyes found her now, commanding the room with
aristocratic aplomb, as if she deemed the attention her
due. Why must she relish looking down her nose at people? Unable to stomach the charade, Lorraine headed for
the room where she'd stored the various bridal shower
favors for the guests. Attendants were scheduled to dis-

tribute them soon, and she wanted to make sure everything was in order.

Moments after she'd entered the coatroom where the favors were stored, the door burst open. Her mother walked in, her body practically vibrating in anger.

"Lorraine, what is the matter with you?" Abigail hissed.

Lorraine sucked in a deep breath, and shook her head. "Not now, Mother."

"Need I remind you that you are at a bridal shower, not a funeral? You will stop this moping at once."

"I'm not getting into this with you right now," Lorraine said. "Go attend to the guests, Mother. I'll be out in a minute."

The set of her mother's jaw was so rigid Lorraine wouldn't be surprised if it broke into a million pieces. Annoyance etched across her face, Abigail pivoted on her designer heels and exited the storage room. Lorraine understood her mother's plight; she was feeling a fair amount of frustration herself.

She turned back to the baskets of shower favors and needlessly straightened them. She needed a few minutes more to collect herself before going back out there.

No, what she really needed was for this shower to be over so that she could go to Carter and smooth things over.

Lorraine felt an immediate stab of guilt. This was her one and only sister's bridal shower, and here she was, hiding out in a closet and counting the seconds until she could leave. She should be out there celebrating with Trina, who had been positively glowing from the moment she'd walked into the tearoom.

There was a soft knock on the door a moment before it opened and her sister walked in. It was that twin thing again. All their lives, all one had to do was think the other's name, and they somehow appeared.

"Hey, you," Trina said. "What's going on? Why are you in here?"

"Just checking on the favors," Lorraine said, motioning to the baskets of crystal wine stoppers and picture frames etched with Trina's and Jackson's names and wedding date.

One of Trina's brows cocked. "Are you expecting them to grow legs and walk out of here?"

Her sister, always the smart-ass.

"Ha-ha," Lorraine said. "I just needed to get away for a bit. My face ached from all of the smiling."

"Now, that I can understand," Trina said.

"How so? Aren't you enjoying yourself? It's the under-the-sea theme, isn't it? You don't like it."

"Would you calm down!" Trina put an arm around Lorraine's shoulders. "I *love* the theme. I was completely floored when I walked in here. And that cake! It's unbelievable."

"Oh, Trina. I'm so happy you like it."

"I didn't say *like*. I said that I *love* it. Thank you so much for all of this." Her sister squeezed her shoulder and pressed a kiss to Lorraine's temple. "Now, can you tell me what's really going on? And not just what has you hiding out in here. I want to know what's been eating at you lately. You haven't been yourself for months, Lorraine."

"Please don't ask. You don't want to know," Lorraine whispered.

"I wouldn't have asked if I didn't want to know. I would just pretend to be blissfully ignorant and ignore the fact that my best friend in the world hasn't been herself lately."

Lorraine stepped out of her sister's grasp and turned to her. "If you really want to know, I'm jealous," she admitted. "Jealous of you and Jackson."

A sad smile pulled at Trina's lips. "I had a feeling that's what you were going to say."

"I'm also…I don't know…hurt? You're leaving me, Trina. Who am I going to turn to when Mother and Father start driving me up the wall?"

"It's not as if I'm moving to the other side of the world, Lorraine. I'll still be here in Chicago, just a few minutes away."

"But with a new husband, and a new life." Lorraine shook her head. "I'm sorry. I'm completely ruining your day. But it's not as if I didn't warn you," she pointed out. "I told you not to ask. You've always been the hard-headed one who never listens."

"Shut up," her sister said, bringing her in for another hug. "You know that I'm always here for you. Always. And you are more than welcome to crash at our place when Abigail and Arnold start driving you crazy. Just promise you'll give Jackson and me a heads-up. We are going to be newlyweds, after all. I wouldn't want you walking in on something you'd rather not see, if you know what I mean."

They both burst out laughing. Count on her silly, down-to-earth sister to brighten her mood.

"Are you ready to go back out there?" Trina asked. "I'm ready to cut that cake so I can find out if it tastes as good as it looks."

"I'll join you in a minute," Lorraine said. She squeezed her sister's hand. "Thanks, Trina."

"Thank *you*," her sister said, enveloping her in a hug. "My shower is absolutely perfect. I love you so much for doing all of this."

Trina started for the door, but stopped with her hand on the doorknob. She turned around. "You know it's just a matter of time, right, Lorraine?"

"A matter of time before what?"

"Before you find someone who makes you as happy as Jackson makes me." Trina winked, and then left the room.

"I may have already found him," Lorraine whispered to herself.

Carter had given her a reason to smile, when she'd had so very little reason to do so in the past few years. He'd awakened her to what life could be like when you were not just going through the motions. She had been so afraid to live—afraid to breathe—in fear of making another mistake that could be detrimental to her family.

But she couldn't go on like this for much longer. She was tired of her parents holding that indiscretion over her head. It had been *five years*. Yes, it had cost them all dearly, and could have cost so much more if the truth had ever come out, but when would it be enough? When would she ever be forgiven and allowed to live her own life?

Lorraine had a feeling that if it were up to her parents, she never would be allowed that luxury.

She was through with making up for that long-ago mistake.

For the next hour she continued to play the perfect hostess alongside her mother, making sure everyone enjoyed themselves. But the entire time Lorraine was mentally counting down the minutes until she could go to Carter. She needed to apologize for her mother. She refused to allow him to think that he wasn't good enough for her, which was exactly what her mother was aiming for with the way she'd treated him.

Lorraine stayed just long enough to bade the final guests goodbye and give Trina the biggest hug she could; then she quickly left the Drake and walked the few blocks to Lillian's.

When she entered the bakery, there was a woman behind the counter this time. She looked a few years younger than Lorraine.

"Welcome to Lillian's," she greeted. "Is there something I can help you with?"

"Yes, I was hoping to speak to Carter."

The woman's brows spiked and her eyes sparkled with recognition. "You're Lorraine Hawthorne-Hayes," she said. "I recognize you from the magazine article in *Chicago Today.* I absolutely love the new chocolate diamonds you were modeling in the magazine."

"Thank you," Lorraine said, concealing a grimace. That magazine spread had been her father's idea.

"I'm Monica Drayson, by the way, Carter's cousin."

"It is very nice to meet you, Monica. Is Carter here?" Lorraine asked, anxious to speak to him.

"Yes, he's in the kitchen. I'll get him." Another person entered the store and Monica held up one finger. "As soon as I take care of this customer," she said.

As she stood among the desserts in the bakery's showroom, Lorraine had to physically stop herself from going into the kitchen and getting Carter herself. No more than three minutes had passed, but it seemed like an hour.

Monica finally returned her attention to Lorraine, saying, "Sorry about that. Let me get Carter."

She left, and a minute later, returned to the showroom…without Carter.

Lorraine's stomach plummeted. Was he going to refuse to see her?

The urge to strangle her mother nearly overwhelmed her, but then the door leading to the back portion of the building swung open and Carter walked out. He was dressed as he was before, but with the added devastating effect of an apron tied around his waist and a smidgen of flour on his cheek. He looked absolutely edible.

"Hello, Carter," Lorraine said, her heart thumping.

"Hi." He crossed his arms over his chest. The defensive stance was not the least bit encouraging.

Lorraine glanced to the right and found his cousin Monica staring unabashedly at them.

"Is there somewhere we can go to talk?" Lorraine asked. "Perhaps that office we visited before, if it's unoccupied?"

He hesitated for a moment, then nodded and motioned for her to follow him. As soon as Carter closed the door to the office, Lorraine started to apologize.

She never got the chance.

Carter spun her around, pinned her against the door and attacked her mouth with a deep, stirring kiss that had her knees weak and her entire body quaking with want. He pushed his tongue past her lips, surging in and out of her mouth with delicious strokes. His hands climbed up her sides, resting next to her breasts for a few moments before covering them. His thumbs grazed her nipples, causing them to pebble despite the barrier her bra and sweater created.

Lorraine glided her hand up to the back of his head, cradling it. She held his head firm, needing to keep it right where it was.

After another full minute, Carter finally ended the assault on her mouth and her senses. He took a step back, his eyes as dazed as she knew her own must be.

"I needed to get that out of the way first," he said, rubbing his hands against his thighs.

"O-okay," Lorraine stammered, a bit dazed.

"How did everything go with your sister's shower?" he asked, much quicker on the recovery than she was.

"Quite well," she said. "Trina was very happy, and everyone loved the cake."

He nodded. "Good."

"Carter—" Lorraine started, but he cut her off.

"Don't worry about it," he said.

"No." She shook her head. "I must apologize for the way my mother treated you. She…" Lorraine decided to be honest. "She is one of the most shallow, self-absorbed people you will ever meet."

"Sounds lovely," he said sardonically.

Lorraine couldn't help feeling horrible for painting her mother in such a light, but it was the truth.

"Carter, my family life is…complicated," she said.

"You think mine isn't?" He laughed, then stretched his hands out, as if trying to encompass the room. "You just stepped into the den of complicated family life. You hear how nice and quiet everything is right now? Just stick around for another twenty minutes or so. It'll be pure chaos."

"Everyone has their share of family drama," she agreed. "I suppose there are varying degrees of it." She took a deep breath, lacing her hands in front of her. "As much as I resent it, I have a certain obligation as a Hawthorne-Hayes. I didn't ask for it. I was born into it, but it's there."

"Which means you can't be seen with a guy who's just a baker? Is that it? Are you trying to tell me that I'm not good enough for you, Lorraine?"

"No!" she practically shouted. "Carter, you are one

of the most amazing people I've ever met. No one has made me laugh the way you do. You are exactly what I need, even though I had no idea how much I needed it."

"So, even though your mother doesn't approve, you're not going to kick me to the curb?"

She stepped up to him and cradled his face in her hands. "Never," she said. "I've had to sacrifice too much of myself already because of my obligations as a Hawthorne-Hayes. I will not sacrifice you, too."

She touched her lips to his in what she'd intended to be an easy, sedate kiss, but she was quickly learning that *easy* and *sedate* were not parts of Carter's vocabulary. The kiss quickly became more heated, and several minutes later, when she was finally able to tear herself away from his tempting mouth, Lorraine had come to a conclusion.

She wanted this man. She wanted him in a way she had never wanted another man. It was more than that; she *deserved* Carter. She'd sacrificed enough; it was time she go after what she really wanted.

"How much longer will you be here at the bakery?" she asked.

"I'm officially off the clock," he told her. "I was putting the finishing touches on my final cake of the day when Monica came in to tell me you were here."

Lorraine took a deep breath. She could do this. She was ready for this.

"In that case, is there somewhere we can go?" she asked. "Somewhere private?"

Lorraine could tell he understood what she was asking by the way his eyes instantly smoldered.

"We could go to my place," he said.

She stared into his eyes, making her feelings known. Then she nodded. Carter grabbed her by the hand and quickly left the office.

Chapter 7

By the time they arrived at his apartment, Carter was practically shaking with anticipation. The thirty-minute drive had taken nearly twice that long because of traffic, but it felt as if it had taken a lifetime. He needed to calm down and get his body under control before he pounced on Lorraine and was finished before they really had the chance to start.

This wasn't him. He took his time, seeing to his partner's pleasure first. Always.

Except, when it came to Lorraine, everything he knew about himself seemed to go out the window. She brought out a side of him he didn't know existed. He craved this woman like no other before her, which was why he needed to make sure he did this right. He needed to slow down, take his time. The fact that he wanted to pin her to the wall as soon as he got her inside made the thought of slowing down unbearable.

Carter unlocked his front door and opened it, gesturing for her to go in ahead of him.

"Welcome to my humble abode."

"Thank you," Lorraine said.

Gone was the temptress who'd boldly asked him to take her somewhere more private. Her smile was shy, her voice barely a whisper. Carter wondered if she would really go through with this. He should prepare himself for the likelihood that he would spontaneously combust if she decided she wasn't ready.

"Your mother would probably say you were slumming it," Carter added with a laugh, but he could tell from Lorraine's instant mood change that it was the wrong thing to say.

"Carter, I'm truly sorry about the way she behaved. Please don't hold it against me."

"No, I'm the one who's sorry. It was a bad joke."

She looked around. "I wouldn't exactly call this slumming it. This apartment is amazing."

By most standards, his apartment was to die for. He was lucky enough to live in one of the Chicago area's most enviable neighborhoods, and had had the place professionally decorated by a sought-after interior designer. It was far more than most men his age could ever hope to afford. But when he tried to see it from Lorraine's eyes, it felt a bit lacking. Compared to that palace overlooking Lake Michigan where she lived, his stylish home really *was* slumming it.

"I must admit that I'm jealous," Lorraine said.

"Why would you be jealous of this? Have you taken a good look at your place?"

"There is a big difference, Carter. It is not *my* place. It's my parents' home."

"But I thought you liked living there?"

Lorraine paused for a moment. "It's not a matter of whether I like or dislike living with my parents. For the most part, I continue to live there because it's what has been expected of me. As I mentioned before, it's complicated. But once Trina leaves, I'm not sure how long I'll be able to go on living there. I'm ready for a change in my life."

"Do I have something to do with that change?" Carter asked.

"You have everything to do with that change," she said, walking up to him and linking her hands behind his head. She looked into his eyes and he saw so much in there: gratitude, acceptance, heat. He loved seeing that heat in her eyes.

"I've spent so much time these past few years trying to be what everyone expects me to be. I lost track of who I really am inside. You've helped me to rediscover the real Lorraine."

"And who *is* the real Lorraine?" he asked. "What does she want?"

"Right now she wants this." Lorraine pulled his head down and touched her lips to his.

The kiss was slow, sensual. Carter's skin tingled, as if being attacked by a million pinpricks. He rubbed his hands up and down Lorraine's sides, finally slipping one up her back and going for the single clasp of her bra. He unhooked it and quickly moved his palms to her breasts, caressing them underneath her sweater.

Lorraine moaned against his mouth, her body relaxing into him.

Carter wanted to continue the slow, sweet kiss, but his body wouldn't allow it. It was screaming for her.

"Let's go to the bedroom," he said.

Once there, he returned to her lips. He couldn't get

enough of her, or how she made him feel with every sexy moan that escaped her throat. She pulled off her sweater and tossed it in a move that was so contradictory to her usually proper demeanor, Carter nearly laughed out loud. But he couldn't get a sound past the thick knot of lust lodged in his throat. Standing before him in nothing but her skirt, she was like a fantasy come to life.

Carter laid her on his bed, following her down, stretching over her body. He bent his head over one breast, pulling the taut peak between his lips as his free hand snaked beneath her skirt. He caught one edge of her panties, and Lorraine caught the other side. Together they pulled the satin down her legs.

Her breaths came in hurried, shallow pants. The sexy sound pulsed in his brain, an aphrodisiac lighting his body on fire.

Carter lifted himself up long enough to grab a condom from the top drawer of the nightstand. He ripped the package open with his teeth, unzipped his pants, pulled himself out and rolled the latex over his erection, his hand shaking in anticipation.

With all the finesse of a sixteen-year-old virgin, he pushed Lorraine's skirt up, spread her legs and entered her.

The heat was unreal. He tried to keep himself still long enough to concentrate on how her incredibly tight body felt wrapped around him, but the compulsion to pump his hips was too great. He moved in and out of her in rapid succession, pistoning his hips, lifting her off the bed with the force of his movement.

Lorraine's arms locked tight around his neck, and her thighs locked even tighter around his waist. Carter buried his head against the curve of her neck, opening his mouth and sucking on her moist, fragrant skin.

After just a few long, strong strokes, he felt Lorraine's body clench around his shaft. She screamed, clawing at his back, her nails biting into his skin even through his shirt.

Carter bit down on her neck as his release rushed out of him. He collapsed on top of her, his shaking limbs unable to hold him up a moment longer. He was completely spent; embarrassingly so.

Shit, he hadn't even pulled his pants down.

"Damn, Lorraine. I'm sorry."

She peered up at him. "Why are you apologizing?"

"Because I'm usually good for more than five minutes," he said, willing his limbs the strength to push off of her. "I've never come that fast before."

He flopped on the bed, his chest heaving with his labored breaths.

"Actually, I believe it was closer to four minutes, but who's watching the clock?" Her teasing laugh floated around the bedroom.

Carter let out a groan. "This is embarrassing."

"Stop it," she admonished. "I'm only teasing you, Carter." She turned onto her side, bracing her chin in her upturned palm. "It was perfect."

"No, it was definitely not perfect," he said, capturing Lorraine's tiny waist and hoisting her up until she straddled his lap. "But give me a few minutes to recover. I'll show you perfect."

An hour later, Carter was certain he was on the verge of cardiac arrest. His heart was beating at such a rapid pace it felt as if it were banging on the walls of his chest. Once again, he found himself flat on his back and staring up at the ceiling as he tried to catch his breath.

"This is excessive," Lorraine blew out on a ragged sigh.

"I think we passed excessive after the third time. I don't know what you would call this."

He levered himself up on one elbow and stared down at her. Her fair skin was flushed from their marathon lovemaking, her cheekbones a delicate pink. With her thick, highlighted hair fanned around her, she looked like a goddess lying there on his sheets.

"Damn, you're beautiful," Carter said, his chest tightening with his swift realization. She was easily one of the sexiest, most beautiful women he'd ever taken to bed. The way her honeyed skin glistened, she seemed almost otherworldly, like an angel sent down from heaven.

Yet, when he'd first laid eyes on her, Carter had dismissed her as not being his type. Nothing had changed about her appearance, so why was he all of a sudden seeing her in such a different light?

An uncomfortable heaviness settled in Carter's chest, weighing him down. He felt an overwhelming need to evade this new, unfamiliar feeling stirring in his gut. He was afraid to examine it, afraid of what he would find if he explored why just the thought of the woman stretched out beside him made his heart ache with tenderness, his pulse quicken with desire.

Why did being with Lorraine feel so different from all the other women he'd taken to bed?

Carter covered his eyes with his forearm and swallowed a groan, determined to block out the four-letter word that throbbed in his brain. This wasn't love. Love didn't happen this quickly. He wasn't convinced it happened at all for some people, himself in particular.

He was the carefree one, the one destined to be like his perpetually single father. If he couldn't get with one woman, another was usually there, waiting in the wings.

Yet, if there was another woman waiting for him,

Carter knew he would dismiss her in an instant. He didn't want anyone else, only the woman lying next to him.

And it scared the hell out of him.

Carter pushed himself up from the bed. The need to put some distance between what had just happened and what he was feeling all but consumed him. He grabbed a pair of sweats and a T-shirt from his drawer and went into the bathroom to clean up and change. When he re-entered his bedroom, Lorraine was sitting up in the bed, covered in a sheet, her hands wrapped around her legs.

They stared at each other for several moments, not saying anything.

"Do you—"

"Perhaps I should—"

Carter gestured for her to go first.

"I was going to say that I should probably return home," she said. "It's late."

Carter remained silent. Something told him that letting her go was the wrong thing to do. They needed to talk, to sort this out. But something even stronger reasoned that letting her go was exactly what he should do. Before he sorted anything out with Lorraine, he first needed to sort it out in his own head.

"Okay," he answered her. Carter thought he saw her flinch, but it was so fleeting he couldn't be sure. "Do you need me to bring you home?"

She pulled in a deep breath, and said, "No. I can call a cab."

"Okay, then." That was definitely hurt that he saw flash across her face. "Wait," he started to say, but Lorraine held her hand up.

"No, it's fine." Her head bobbed with a curt nod. "I'm fine."

She pushed up from the bed, picked her clothes up from the floor and went into the bathroom. Carter walked to the kitchen and grabbed a bottle of water from the fridge. He leaned against the counter and gulped down half of it.

He was being an asshole.

But he didn't know what else to do. This was uncharted territory, and it was seriously scaring the hell out of him. He didn't do the emotional stuff. He didn't know how to make it all work. Just look at the role model he'd had. Devon Drayson, Mr. Noncommitment.

Lorraine emerged from his bedroom, dressed in the cream-colored suit she'd worn to her sister's bridal shower, and looking as if she'd just stepped out of a boardroom instead of a bedroom.

Carter grabbed his keys. "I'll drive you home."

"No." She held up her cell phone. "I've already called a cab. They should be downstairs by the time I get there."

Don't let her take the cab, his conscience demanded. But he dropped the keys back onto the counter.

Lorraine stared at the keys, then at him. In a shallow voice, she said, "Good night, Carter."

He swallowed past the uncomfortable lump clogging his throat. "Good night," he managed to get out.

And he let her go.

Lorraine unlocked the door to the penthouse, walked inside and yelped.

"Where have you been?" her mother demanded.

She clutched a hand to her chest. "My goodness, Mother. You scared me half to death."

"You've been with that baker," her mother said, her voice oozing accusation and reproach.

"Would you please stop referring to him as 'that baker'? He is more than just a baker."

"What a relief to know that my daughter doesn't wrap her arms around just anyone. Although I certainly do not approve of the way you let him kiss you, as if there was no one else around."

"Oh, for goodness' sake, Mother, it's not as if we started doing it in front of you."

"Lorraine!"

"His name is Carter Drayson," she said over her mother's shriek. "He is the head artisan cake baker at Lillian's."

"Yes, he imparted that much when he delivered Trina's cake. But I don't care what kind of cakes he bakes, he is still *just* a baker, Lorraine."

"He is also the grandson of Lillian and Henry Drayson, the same Draysons who own that building on Michigan Avenue and that huge estate in Glenville Heights, along with several other properties around the city."

Just that quickly, her mother's entire demeanor changed. Lorraine felt physically ill. How could anyone be so shamelessly shallow?

"You are unbelievable," Lorraine said. "Now that you know he is from a wealthy family, Carter is suddenly acceptable in your eyes?"

"I did not say he was acceptable," Abigail hissed. She lifted her chin in the air. "But it does make a difference. If he has his own money, he won't be after yours. I gather this is the same man you were plastered against in the newspaper? Stuart showed me the photo."

Count on her brother to not mention it to her, but to go straight to their parents.

"Mother, just leave this alone. Please. I like Carter. He likes me. It shouldn't matter that he's a Drayson."

"Someone needs to look out for you, Lorraine. You don't always make the wisest choices when it comes to men."

"I am not an imbecile. Yes, I made a horrible mistake five years ago. But do you know what is so wonderful about mistakes, Mother? A person can learn from them."

"And have you?" her mother charged. "Have you really learned, Lorraine? Or did you let yourself get swept up in this Carter person before you even knew who he really was?"

"Why does that matter? Even if Carter really was just a baker at Lillian's, it should not matter. Not every man is like Broderick." She pointed an accusing finger at her mother. "You had no right to treat Carter the way you did today."

"I had every right. I was looking out for you."

"I am not a child. I don't need you to look out for me."

Her mother clenched her lips and jutted out her jaw. "Fine. I was looking out for the Hawthorne-Hayes name. You tend to forget that what you do has consequences not only for you, but for this entire family. I will not allow you to bring shame upon this family again."

Lorraine closed her eyes. She sucked in a deep breath and warily blew it out. "How many times will I have to apologize?"

"You've apologized enough. You need to demonstrate how sorry you are by not making those same stupid choices again."

"I am not going to stop seeing Carter," Lorraine stated, her tone resolute.

"Fine," her mother said again. "But if he turns out to be just like that other bastard, don't run to me and your father to bail you out. Is that clear?"

Lorraine held her head up. "Crystal clear."

Her mother subjected her to her most superior stare, the one Lorraine had witnessed throughout her childhood. She knew better than to be fooled by the outwardly calm expression; Lorraine could tell by the slight flare of her nostrils that Abigail was beyond enraged. Part of it was more than likely due to her lack of control over the situation. Her mother thrived on controlling every aspect of her family.

But Lorraine also acknowledged that some of Abigail's vehemence was warranted. When it came to Carter's integrity and motives, all her mother had to go on was Lorraine's judgment, which, admittedly, had been flawed in the past. Other than Lorraine's word, Abigail had no way of knowing if Carter's intentions were honorable. For that matter, neither did Lorraine.

After tonight, she wasn't so sure of his intentions, either.

She went into her bedroom, trying to block the feelings of uncertainty that clawed up her throat as she recalled Carter's change in demeanor after they'd made love. He'd pulled away, both physically and emotionally. It had been so long since she'd been intimate with a man that Lorraine hadn't been sure exactly what to expect, but she certainly had not anticipated his distant, almost cold reaction.

Was Carter just looking for sex, and now that he'd gotten it, was he done? Had she foolishly allowed herself to be used again?

She stared into her bathroom mirror, unsure what to think of the woman staring back at her. Maybe her mother was right. Maybe she just was not capable of making sound choices when it came to men.

"I trusted you, Carter Drayson," Lorraine whispered. "Please don't make me regret it."

Chapter 8

"Dammit!"

Carter put his hands on his hips and stared at the entire bowl of buttercream frosting splattered across the floor.

"What's going on with you?" Malik asked, walking up to him. "First you overcook the lemon filling, and now this?"

Carter grabbed a towel from the counter and started cleaning up the mess. "I'm just tired," he said. Malik's chuckle grated on his nerves. He looked over his shoulder. "What's so damn funny?"

"You've got it bad" was Malik's response.

"You don't know what you're talking about," Carter said as he flung the icing into a trash bin.

"Remember who you're talking to. It wasn't all that long ago that I was in your shoes. Stop trying to fight it, Carter. It's no use. You're caught."

"Nobody has caught me," he said. "I'm not like you. This thing with Lorraine is just… We're just having fun."

Even as he said it, Carter wanted to take back the words. They left a vile taste in his mouth. He didn't want to cheapen what he'd found with Lorraine, despite the fact that it scared the hell out of him.

"Does she know that?" Malik asked. "Actually, a better question is, do *you* know that? Because from where I'm standing, you're doing more than just having a little fun. I've never seen you like this before."

He'd never felt like this before, and that was what frightened him the most.

He'd had his share of women. Actually, he'd had his, his cousins' and the entire Chicago White Sox outfield's share of women. But never had he fallen so deeply, so quickly and so damn hard. He didn't do long-term and high emotion. He did carefree and easy exits.

Not this time. This time, he had no desire to make a run for it.

Carter couldn't shake the guilt he felt over allowing Lorraine to leave last night. It was bad enough that he hadn't taken her home, but he hadn't even walked her downstairs to meet the cab. What in the hell was wrong with him?

He pulled out his cell phone, but his fingers just hovered. He couldn't bring himself to call her.

Coward.

He'd attempted this call at least a half dozen times since she'd left last night, but had yet to follow through. He was still unsure of what to say to her. Should he come right out and apologize? Should he play it off as though he didn't think he had anything to atone for?

He was so out of his element on this one it wasn't even funny.

Phone call or not, he had to do something to let her know he was thinking of her. Because he *was* thinking of her. Constantly.

Carter pulled up the internet browser on his cell phone and searched for a local florist. He was about to order a dozen roses when he remembered their walk along the Nature Boardwalk the night of the event at Lincoln Park Zoo. He changed his order to irises.

Carter knew this did nothing to make up for how he'd left things last night, but he could only hope that it was a start on his road to forgiveness.

He returned to scraping up icing with a spatula, and spotted Shari's son, Andre, standing in the corner, watching him.

"Hey there, little man." Carter motioned for him to come over. He'd always felt a kinship with Andre that he'd never felt with the rest of his cousins. Maybe it was because he had something in common with the four-year-old that his other cousins couldn't relate to. Like Carter, Andre knew what it was like to grow up with a single mom.

But at least Carter had his dad. Thomas Abernathy, Andre's dad, had left Shari after she'd told him about the pregnancy, and hadn't been heard from since. It was Thomas's loss; Andre was a pretty cool kid.

"How's it going?" Carter asked him.

Andre shrugged. "I want a cupcake, but Mommy told me I can't have any more sugar today."

"You're in a bakery. You can't help having sugar." Carter looked around. "Come on." He motioned for Andre to follow him to the refrigerated storage units where they stored the pastries. "Chocolate or straw-berry?" he asked him.

"Strawberry," he said, his green eyes sparkling in mischievous delight.

Carter retrieved a strawberry and cream cupcake and handed it to Andre. He put a finger to his lips.

"Shh…"

"Okay," Andre mouthed, taking a big bite out of his cupcake. He smiled up at him, those twin dimples dotting the corners of his mouth.

Carter was envious of the kid. He'd give anything to go back to the days when a cupcake made everything better.

But it would take a lot more than a sweet treat to resolve his current problems. Although, now that he thought about it, sweets couldn't hurt.

Carter went into the retail shop and ordered a dozen gourmet cupcakes to be delivered to Lorraine's, to go along with the irises he'd sent. Cupcakes wouldn't make up for his callousness last night, but at this point, Carter needed all the help he could get.

He checked his watch. He and his cousins were scheduled to have a powwow to discuss *You Take the Cake* in a couple of minutes. Carter looked around the retail shop to make sure everything was running smoothly, and then headed for the back. As he was making his way down the hallway, he ran into Belinda and Malik coming out of the storage room.

Carter lifted his hands, staving off comment. "I don't even want to know."

"Hey, don't knock it till you try it," Malik said.

Belinda slapped his arm. "We were restocking the shelves with the shipment of cake boxes that just arrived."

Malik winked. "Restocking the shelves. That's our code name for you know what."

That earned him another slap from Belinda, followed by a kiss. Carter felt the urge to throw up. He followed his cousin and his best friend into the largest office, where the rest of his cousins were seated.

Drake had his computer screen hooked up to a projector, which illuminated one wall.

"Is everybody ready?" he asked.

"What's this meeting for again?" Malik asked.

"We need to brainstorm our game plan for *You Take the Cake,*" Shari said. She looked pointedly at Carter. "I'm going to get you for giving my son that cupcake."

"Lighten up," Carter said. "Every kid needs a cupcake every now and then. So," he addressed the rest of the room. "I thought the game plan was annihilating Brown Sugar Bakery?"

"That sounds like a plan to me," Drake agreed.

"That is *not* the plan," Monica said. "I'm sure the show's producers would love the side drama, but I refuse to provide it. We will be representing Lillian's, and that's not what Lillian's is about."

Count on his youngest cousin to have the most level head, Carter thought.

"Monica is right," Belinda interjected. "This competition is about more than just beating Dina's bakery. It's our chance to really put Lillian's on the map—not just in Illinois but across the country. We're already getting national and even some international orders for our prepackaged bake mixes, and the local grocery stores that currently carry our baked goods have all been increasing their orders. If we win *You Take the Cake,* we would be in position to expand these two segments of the business exponentially."

"We've already decided that one way to stand out from the competition is to incorporate some really out-of-the-box flavors," Monica said. "I've been working on a lemon poppy seed and rhubarb cupcake that is to die for."

"She's right," Shari said. "I tried it, and I nearly died because it was so bad."

Monica stuck her tongue out at her sister.

"It's not just the flavors," Carter said. "One-third of the judges' scores are based on the decorations. If we want to stand out, we'll have to bring it. I just ordered some food-grade platinum glitter dust for the Eiffel Tower on the France cake. If I can find the extra time this week I'm going to practice by making a smaller version."

"I'm not worried about decorations." This from Belinda. "After that cake you did for the Hawthorne-Hayes bridal shower, I think you can do just about anything, Carter."

"Yeah, you brought your A game with that one," Malik said. "How did they like the cake?"

All eyes turned to him. Carter tried for nonchalant. "They liked it."

"That's all?" Monica asked.

"Yeah." He shrugged.

"He's holding back on us," Drake said. "You can stop with the mysteriousness. We all saw the paper. I never pegged you for falling for someone as uptight as a Hawthorne-Hayes, though."

"According to Carter, they're just 'having fun.'" Malik made air quotes with his fingers.

"Didn't look that way from what I saw in the newspaper," Monica said. "Or what Amber said she saw the other night at Lincoln Park Zoo. Apparently, things got hot and heavy."

Carter could feel his cheeks burning. "Can we get back to discussing the TV show?"

He glanced over at Shari, who was looking at him with a concerned, haunting expression on her face.

"Well, even though some of you may think the Dina situation isn't that important, I disagree," Drake said. "We need to talk about how we're going to handle it. I say we call her out on national television for being a lying bitch."

"Grandma Lillian would have a fit," Belinda pointed out.

Carter replied, "We can't let her just get away with what she did. Everything she's doing in that bakery comes from what she learned here."

"She's already gotten away with it," Belinda countered.

Carter nodded. "And that's why we need to call her on it."

Malik stopped the argument and looked to Shari. "She was your best friend, Shari. How do you think we should handle her?"

Shari looked at them all. Then she cradled her face in her hands, said, "I can't do this" and ran out of the room.

"Let her go," Drake said.

But Carter wouldn't. He couldn't. He got up and went after Shari, finding her standing in the alcove between the storage room and the first consultation office.

"Hey," Carter said as he approached her. "You okay?"

She wiped at the fresh tears streaming down her cheeks. "I'm fine," Shari said.

"I don't think so." Cautiously, he reached out and stroked her arm. "What's going on, Shari? I know you were hurt when Dina backstabbed everyone, but you shouldn't let it upset you just because she was your friend."

"I brought her into the business," Shari said.

"So? I brought Malik in. If he'd turned out to be a backstabbing asshole, I wouldn't see it as totally my fault." Although, when he thought about it, Carter realized that he would indeed have felt a measure of guilt. He finally understood what his cousin was going through.

"Look," he said, capturing Shari's shoulders and giving them a reassuring squeeze. "What's done is done. You had no idea Dina would backstab us all." He paused, then asked, "Did you?"

"Carter!" Shari gasped.

"I'm sorry. I should have known better than to ask that."

"Yes, you should have." Shari sniffed and wiped her eyes again.

"Hey, you still haven't chewed me out for giving Andre that cupcake. You can do that if it'll make you feel better."

His cousin laughed. "I should, but I won't. Let him have his cupcake. At least one person in this family should be happy."

Carter's chest tightened at the sadness on his cousin's face. He understood her guilt, but this seemed excessive. "Shari, what's really going on? Why wouldn't you be happy?"

"Don't worry about it." She shook her head, and then her eyes focused on his face. "Now, you tell me something. Are *you* happy? With Lorraine, I mean."

Carter dropped his hands and took a step back.

"It isn't hard to see, Carter. You've been walking

around here for the past couple of weeks looking as if you've won the lottery."

"Maybe I did and just didn't tell anyone."

"You didn't win the lottery. You're in love."

Carter instantly recoiled at his cousin's assessment. "Now you're starting to sound like Malik. After what you went through with Andre's dad, I thought you'd know better."

A dark shadow clouded over Shari's face, and Carter felt like the biggest jerk in all of Chicago. "I'm sorry for bringing up Thomas," he said.

Shari pulled in a shaky breath. "It's okay. Just promise me one thing, Carter. Be careful with her heart. Don't lead Lorraine on. If you're not serious about her, you should end it before she ends up getting hurt."

Carter was disturbed by the haunted look in his cousin's eyes. After all these years, he wouldn't have thought Shari was still so affected by Thomas Abernathy's betrayal, but apparently she was.

"I won't hurt her," he promised Shari.

She gave him a peck on the cheek. "Thanks for caring enough to check on me. Now, why don't we go back and figure out how we're going to win this competition? Because Drake is right—I want to kick Dina's butt."

"Hand me a few of those hydrangeas," Francine called.

Lorraine picked up a handful of colorful hydrangeas from the array of flowers scattered about the large table, and brought them over to Francine. Nearly every week since she was eight years old, Lorraine had spent her Saturday afternoons helping Frannie put together the fresh flower arrangements that adorned the tables and mantelpieces around the penthouse throughout the week.

Her mother had balked at the idea of Lorraine doing such a menial task, but Lorraine had ignored her. The bright colors and artistry of the flower arranging called to her creative side.

"That's beautiful," she told Frannie, gesturing to the enormous spray of eucalypti, hydrangeas and lilies.

"Not as beautiful as those." Frannie looked pointedly at the vase filled with lovely irises that had been delivered a few hours ago, followed almost immediately by a box of decadent cupcakes in the signature pink-and-brown-striped box from Lillian's.

She couldn't deny the thrill she'd experienced when the flowers and cupcakes had arrived, but her joy was diminished by the fact that they had not been accompanied by a phone call. Lorraine was still hurt that Carter had allowed her to leave last night. He hadn't just allowed her to leave. He'd looked…relieved.

She'd spent the morning vacillating between shock and fury. Until those flowers had arrived, she'd had the sinking feeling that she had been misled again, deluded into thinking that a man had actually cared for her, when all he'd wanted was something from her.

The gifts had momentarily appeased her, but Lorraine was still hurt. Could he not call? Send a text?

Perhaps he was in the middle of creating some gargantuan cake?

But surely he could step away for a moment to send her a simple "how are you doing?" text message.

Goodness, was she really pining away while waiting for a phone call? What was she? Twelve?

"He'll call," Frannie said.

Lorraine blinked. "Excuse me?"

"You've never been good at hiding what you're think-ing. I said that he will call." Frannie sent her a sly smile. "He makes you happy, doesn't he? It's been a long time since I've seen you smile as much as you have these past couple of weeks. It looks good on you."

"I didn't realize I was such an open book," Lorraine said.

"Remember that I've known you since you were born. It's hard to keep things hidden from me."

Frannie probably knew her better than her own mother did. She'd certainly spent more time caring for Lorraine and Trina than Abigail ever had.

"Here's my question," Frannie said. She gave Lor-raine a pointed look. "What's stopping you from call-ing him?"

"You think *I* should call *him?*"

"Your hand isn't broken, is it?"

"No." Lorraine laughed. She dropped the shears and removed her gloves. Then she leaned over and kissed Frannie's cheek. "Thank you."

"Anytime," her housekeeper answered.

Lorraine went into the solarium—her favorite quiet place in the penthouse—and sat on the bench next to a potted banana tree. She pulled out her phone and, be-fore she lost her nerve, punched in Carter's number. She would not read anything into it if he didn't pick up. Maybe he was busy. Maybe he was—

"Hello?" He picked up on the third ring. "Lorraine?"

She expelled a relieved breath. "Hello, Carter. I hope I'm not disturbing you."

"No, no. I'm just at the bakery, as usual."

"In the middle of decorating another masterpiece?" she asked, almost hopeful.

"No, no big decorating jobs on tap for today."

Anger and disappointment inundated her at his admission. If he hadn't been elbow deep in buttercream frosting and fancy sugared flowers, why hadn't he called her?

"The family just finished a meeting about *You Take the Cake*," he further explained. For a moment, Lorraine wondered if she'd ranted aloud.

"The competition is getting close," she said, his explanation abating her anger. At least to a degree.

"Yeah, next month." The tension that stretched across the phone lines was palpable. Lorraine could hear her heartbeat pounding in her ears.

When Carter spoke again, his voice was drenched in apology.

"Lorraine, I'm sorry about last night. Not for what we did," he quickly interjected. "But I'm sorry for the way I acted after. I was…confused."

"Confused?" she asked. "We had sex and you sent me home. There is nothing confusing about that, Carter," Lorraine softly accused. She'd dropped her voice to nearly a whisper. She wasn't sure if she'd done it so that Frannie wouldn't overhear her, or simply because it hurt too much to hear the words.

"God, Lorraine. I'm *so* sorry."

"So am I," she said.

"I knew I was being an asshole. I just didn't know… I'm not used to…"

Lorraine could practically feel the frustration coming through his voice.

"Look, this is really hard to explain over the phone. Do you maybe want to come over to my place?"

She was quiet for such a long stretch of time that Carter asked, "Lorraine, are you still there?"

For a moment she thought about hanging up the

phone, but then she thought about how miserable she'd been since leaving his apartment last night. Only a portion of that misery had been caused by his callousness in letting her go; much of it had to do with how much she'd missed talking to him today.

"I can be there in an hour," she finally answered.

Carter's relieved sigh should have made her feel better. Instead, Lorraine recalled the look on his face as she'd closed the door to his apartment last night. He'd looked relieved then, too.

Carter wasn't the only one confused here. She wasn't sure what to think anymore, but she knew what she'd felt over these past couple of weeks. She'd felt alive. For the first time in a very long while, she'd felt pure, sweet joy, all thanks to Carter. She owed it to herself to hear him out.

Chapter 9

Carter had been pacing back and forth in the space between his kitchen island and the sink trying to figure out just what to say to Lorraine when she arrived. Thank God he'd convinced her to come over. Those several long moments when she hadn't responded to his request had been some of the most agonizing he'd ever endured.

"This is crazy," Carter said to the empty room.

When had he ever been this messed up in the head over a woman? He'd hooked up, and then broken up, with dozens of women in the past. Why was this one so different? And why did it feel as if his world had ended when he thought he'd ruined things with her?

A soft knock halted his pacing. Carter rushed to the door and yanked it open, a sweet ache settling in his chest when he found Lorraine standing in the hallway. God, she looked lovely. And vulnerable. And kissable.

But he didn't have the right to pull her in and kiss her until neither of them could breathe. He owed her a real apology first, and an explanation.

If only he could figure out why he'd acted like the jackass of the century.

"Thanks for coming over," Carter said, stepping aside so that she could enter the apartment.

She remained silent as she stepped inside, walking to the other end of the kitchen. She didn't even take off the purse hanging on her shoulder. She looked as if she was ready to flee at any moment.

"Can I get you something to drink?" he asked. "A glass of wine? Soda?"

"No, thank you," she finally said, her sweet, gentle voice flowing over him like honey.

Carter couldn't keep up the nonchalant act another minute. "God, Lorraine, I'm so damn sorry for the way I treated you last night," he said, making it to her in three strides. He captured her hands between his. "Last night was unlike anything I've ever felt before." His face contorted in a grimace. "Damn, I sound like Malik."

"Who?"

"Never mind." He brought her fingers to his lips. "Lorraine, I've been with my share of women." Another grimace. "Wait, that didn't come out right."

"I had no illusions that you were pure and innocent, Carter. I could tell from the second I met you what kind of guy you were."

Her words caused something ugly to churn in his gut. He'd always worn his player status like a badge of honor, but he didn't like the thought of Lorraine seeing him that way. He wanted to be better than that for her.

"Perhaps we should slow this down a bit," she said. "Maybe it's all moving too fast."

"It is moving fast, but it feels…it feels *right,* Lorraine." He brought a hand up to cradle her jaw. Her skin was so soft, so damn lovely. Carter looked her in the eye, willing her to understand. "I haven't been a choirboy—not by a long shot. But I have never, ever felt the way I felt last night. When I was with you, it was… I can't even describe it. It scared me, Lorraine. I've never felt that way with a woman before."

"You're not the only one who's scared, Carter. This is new for me, too. I've spent such a long time guarding my heart, and every time I'm with you, you chip away at my armor." She pulled her bottom lip between her teeth. In a hushed voice, she said, "I don't want to get hurt."

"I won't hurt you." Carter shook his head. "I promise you."

Unable to stop himself, he leaned in and pressed his lips against hers. It felt like coming home. He could count on his fingers just how many times he'd kissed this woman, yet, just this quickly, she was home to him.

Carter brought both hands up, cupping her jaw in one, her soft, warm cheek in the other. He slid his fingers into her silky hair, holding her head in place as he licked along the seam of her lips and gently worked his tongue inside.

She tasted like pure heaven. His body was screaming for him to pick her up and carry her to his bed, but he didn't deserve it, not after the way he'd treated her last night. Settling for just her kisses would be his penance. It was the kind of penance any sinner would give his soul for.

An hour later, they were nestled together on his sofa, watching a rerun of last year's season of *You Take the Cake.*

"I am amazed at what people can do with cake," Lorraine said.

"You just have to have a plan and a steady hand," Carter said. "I sketch everything out first so I know exactly what I'm going to do before I put the first cake in the oven."

"How many cakes would it take to make something like that?" she asked, motioning to the cake that was made to look like Tara from *Gone with the Wind*.

"Probably eight to ten. It all starts out as one huge block, with all of the cakes stacked one on top of the other, and then you just carve away at it, like a sculptor with a block of clay."

She looked up at him. "You really are an artist."

Carter shrugged. "In a way."

"So, when Lillian's wins the competition, how will all of you split the prize money?"

"It'll go back into the business. It isn't about the prize money. It's all about exposure. We've got some huge expansion ideas for the bakery, and just having the opportunity to be on a nationally televised show will bring recognition to the brand."

She looked up at him again over her shoulder and, with a sly smile, said, "But you want to win, don't you?"

"Oh, yeah," Carter admitted. "I want to win *so* bad, especially because of who we're competing against."

"Who's the competition?"

"There are three additional bakeries in the competition, including Brown Sugar Bakery," he said, unable to keep the loathing from his voice.

"I get the sense that there's a story there."

"More like a nightmare," Carter said with a huff. He brought Lorraine's back closer to his chest and wrapped his arms around her. "Brown Sugar Bakery is owned by onetime Lillian's employee Dina English. She and my cousin Shari used to be best friends."

"*Used* to be?"

He nodded. "Dina spent as much time in the bakery as the rest of us grandkids, so it was no surprise when she started working there. It *was* a surprise when she up and quit and started her own bakery, with some recipes that were very similar to Grandma Lillian's."

"She stole your grandmother's recipes?"

"She says she didn't. And she was smart enough to tweak them just enough so that they are not exactly the same, but that doesn't mean all that much to me or the rest of the family. Dina stabbed us all in the back, as far as I'm concerned."

"Your cousin must feel awful."

He sighed, thinking of his conversation with Shari after their last family meeting. "That's the hardest part. Shari feels responsible. She shouldn't. I mean, how could she have known that Dina would do what she did?"

"I can understand how she must feel. It's not easy to get over the fact that you've caused your family harm, even when it was completely by accident."

Carter noted the change in her tone of voice. "Are you speaking from experience?"

She looked up at him, and he could tell that she was. "I don't want to get into that right now." She snuggled closer to him. "I just want to hang out like a regular person. This is wonderful, Carter. And very rare for me."

"Why is that?"

She shrugged. "I always have to watch what I say and do. One misstep and it can mean disaster for the Hawthorne-Hayeses' standing in society."

"How do you stay sane with everyone always in your

business?" he asked. He got some noteworthiness as a Drayson, but just in these short couple of weeks he'd been with Lorraine, he could tell that she had to work hard to maintain her privacy.

"I've lived with it my entire life, so in some ways I'm used to it."

"I don't know if I could ever get used to having to constantly watch what I say, or wondering if I'm going to be on the front page of the newspaper."

"It keeps me on my toes. It's why I never leave the house without makeup," she said with a light laugh, but Carter heard the note of exasperation behind it.

"It seems exhausting, always having to be on."

"That's why tonight is such a treat. I can't remember the last time I lounged on a sofa and watched television."

"I'm happy you're enjoying it," he said. "I think you need to do more things that are just for you."

After a pause, she said, "Actually, I do." She twisted around in his arms, resting her chin on his chest and looking up at him. "I want to take you somewhere."

"Where?"

She levered herself up from the sofa and held her hand out to him. "Don't ask, just follow."

If any other woman had issued that command, Carter would have balked. With Lorraine, he didn't even hesitate.

Lorraine spent the entire drive from Glenville Heights to Wicker Park trying to decide if she should take a detour and go somewhere else. Was she ready to share this part of herself with Carter?

Other than her sister, and a few of her friends in the arts community, no one else knew of the loft she owned in this area of Chicago.

"What are we doing out here?" Carter asked when she parked along the street, a block away from her building.

"As I told you earlier, I have something to show you," she said. They entered the building and she motioned for him to follow her up to the third floor. The entire time, Lorraine's heart pounded against her rib cage. What if he took one look at her paintings and laughed?

Carter wouldn't do such a thing. Also, it shouldn't matter whether he fawned all over her paintings, either. She had enough confidence in her work that it didn't matter what his reaction was.

If that's the case, why are you bringing him here?

Their arrival to her third-story loft put an abrupt end to her mental debate. Taking a deep breath, Lorraine opened the door and stepped aside so he could enter ahead of her. Ever the gentleman, Carter refused to take one step. She shook her head at his gallantry.

"Such manners," Lorraine teased.

"I'm Lillian Drayson's grandson. I wouldn't dream of letting it get out that I walked into a room ahead of a woman. That's just asking for a slap upside the head."

She chuckled at that mental picture. Before turning the light on, Lorraine turned to him and said, "It is costing me a lot to share this with you, Carter. This is a part of myself that I rarely show people, but I feel as if I can trust you with it." She flipped the switch next to the door, and the vast room was illuminated in bright lights.

Carter stepped farther into the space and moved in a slow circle, taking in everything before him. "Is this an art studio?" he asked, motioning to the canvases leaning against the wall.

"Yes. *My* art studio," Lorraine answered. "I paint."

Carter walked over to the closest gathering of canvases.

"Not all of these are finished," Lorraine quickly pointed out.

He reached for her painting of St. Mary of the Angels Church in neighboring Bucktown, then snatched his hand back. He looked over at her. "Can I?"

Lorraine nodded. She pulled her bottom lip between her teeth, her nerves on edge.

"This is incredible. I think I recognize the building." He looked up at her. "It's the big church on Hermitage, right?"

"Yes." She stepped forward, stood next to him.

"Something about this style looks familiar, the way the brushstrokes all slant at this angle."

Lorraine sucked in a quick breath. Did he know?

"The style is similar to another artist whose work I follow, but she's not known for painting religious buildings. Far from it."

Suddenly his entire body became rigid. He looked at her, his eyes widening in disbelief. Carter peered closer at the painting of the Polish-style cathedral. He picked up another painting and did the same. Then another.

Lorraine could practically see the pieces falling into place in his mind.

"You said your middle name is Elise," he said slowly.

She pulled her bottom lip between her teeth and nodded.

"You've got to be kidding me. *You're* L. Elise?"

"In the flesh," she said.

"The flesh is right. That's just what comes to mind when I think of L. Elise. Where are *those* paintings, the real ones?"

"These paintings are real," Lorraine said with a nervous chuckle. "But you are talking about the ones over there." She gestured toward the far right side of the loft. A long white curtain hung from the high ceiling and stretched the length of the room.

Carter headed straight for it, moved the curtain aside and let out a long whistle. "Now, *this* is what L. Elise is known for."

Lorraine stood next to him and studied the paintings. To say they were provocative was an understatement. They ran the gamut, from a portrait of a well-defined male torso, to a couple in the throes of making love. For Lorraine, it wasn't about the erotic image as much as it was about capturing the passion and emotion of the moment. Her work had been praised by art critics around Chicago for giving credence to erotic art.

Carter held up a canvas and studied it. His eyes narrowed. His head tilted to one side. "I give up. What exactly is this? It's beautiful," he added quickly. "I just can't figure out what it is."

"I'll give you a hint. It's called *Chante's Dinner Table*," she said. "Does that help?"

He studied it a bit longer. "Nope."

"Chante is my friend Bianca's baby girl, and the painting is of Bianca's left breast. Hence the name, Chante's Dinner Table."

He looked close. "That's a nipple!" he said, as if he'd discovered the Holy Grail. "You actually got your friend to pose for this?"

"As long as I didn't use her face or name, she was fine with it. I seldom hire actual models. The majority of my subjects are friends I've made in the art world."

"Have you posed for other artists?" he asked.

"Yes, but I'll never disclose which paintings. I made sure there was no way to identify me."

Carter's gaze instantly smoldered. "So, no paintings of the raspberry-shaped birthmark on your hip?" He shook his head. "There are more sides to you than I ever imagined, Lorraine Elise."

Her cheeks flamed with embarrassment and a bombardment of heat. "This only scratches the surface," she told him.

That brought even more heat to his eyes, but he turned his attention back to her paintings.

"Let me see if I've got this one right. It's a woman lying down on her side."

"Correct," Lorraine said, impressed. "What you see there is the rise of her hip. It swoops down into the bend of her waist. She was against a bluish backdrop, so the painting appears more like the sky over sweeping plains than a woman's naked torso."

"Very clever."

"That's the point. I think erotic paintings are even more provocative when it's not in your face. You should have to really study it."

The next painting he picked up was of a man with rippling muscles bent over a naked woman. His head was cushioned between her thighs. The woman's back was arched, and her hand held one of her breasts.

"Perhaps that particular painting is a bit more in your face," Lorraine conceded.

"It's all in his face," Carter remarked. "How did you get them to hold that pose?"

"I didn't have models for that painting. It was done by imagination only."

"Mmm…just imagine if you had the real thing," he said, setting the painting back against the wall.

Lorraine knew she was playing with fire. She knew

exactly what Carter was trying to do. Yet she still asked, "Are you volunteering?"

"What do you think?" he said before claiming her mouth.

Never leaving each other's lips, they backed their way to the raised dais in the center of the room. It was still draped in the deep purple silks that her model had lounged upon for the painting she was currently working on.

Carter followed her down, cradling the back of her head in his hand as his tongue plundered her mouth. He worked his way down her neck, chest and torso, peppering her shirt with kisses before lifting it up and over her head.

As she lay before him, Lorraine was happy she'd chosen her hot-pink lace bra and panty set. It was a contrast to the straitlaced image she'd been required to uphold on the outside, a small nod to the girl with a rebellious streak. She missed that girl. Carter had helped her to find her again.

He hovered above her, straddling her hips. He leaned over and ran his tongue from the valley between her breasts down to her belly button, where another mark of that rebellious girl lay hidden.

Carter looked up at her. "A belly button ring?"

She nodded, a grin tilting her lips.

"Why didn't I see that last night?"

"Because I didn't have it in last night. I stopped wearing it for a while."

She'd had the belly button ring put back in just this morning. She'd started feeling more like the old Lorraine, the one she'd missed so much.

"I like it," he said, then dipped his head and flicked at the solitary diamond stud with his tongue. "Is this the only hidden piercing, or will I find something else if I go exploring farther south?"

She wanted to tell him to find out for himself, but she wasn't that bold yet. Or…maybe she was.

"You won't find any more piercings, but don't let that stop you from exploring."

He looked up at her with a smile so wicked it caused all kinds of naughty tremors to race along her skin. Carter hooked his thumbs into the waistband of her skirt and tugged it down her waist. Lorraine lifted the small of her back from the dais so that he could pull the material over her hips and down her legs.

He traveled back up her body, pressing a kiss to the damp lace between her legs.

She couldn't hold back the moan that escaped her throat. Having him kiss the barrier between them was almost as erotic as having his lips on her bare skin.

Almost.

She peeled her panties from her hips and pushed them to her knees. Carter took care of the rest, tugging the lace down her legs and then capturing her knees. He spread them wide and pressed a kiss to each side of her inner thighs.

"Know what I think?" Carter whispered.

"What?" she gasped.

"I think we should re-create that scene from your painting."

Lorraine pitched her head back. "I'd…I'd like that."

Just as in the painting, her left hand came up to caress her breast, still covered in the hot-pink lace. The rasp of the fabric against her swollen nipple was pleasure-filled pain. Her other hand clasped Carter's head, urging him to continue the glorious feats his tongue was performing between her legs. He was relentless, going from rapid flicks of his tongue to long, languid licks.

Lorraine bit her bottom lip, trying to hold back from the climax that was steadily building within her. Carter pinched the nub of nerves at her cleft just as his tongue invaded her, and her entire world exploded. Her body shook with violent tremors as pleasure coursed throughout her bloodstream, yet Carter refused to relent. He continued his sensual assault, bringing her to another climax just moments after the first.

Lorraine collapsed onto the silken drape, her limbs liquid, her entire being sated.

But Carter was not done. In fact, from the wicked gleam in his eyes, he was only getting started.

Despite the erection straining against the fly of his jeans, Carter kept his pants zipped. He knew if he were to take them off now, he would be inside Lorraine in a hot second. He wanted to prolong this for as long as possible, to make up for the way he'd sent her home last night.

He levered himself up and knelt before her. She looked like an erotic fantasy draped across all that satiny deep purple fabric. It flowed around her like a dark, turbulent ocean.

And was there anything sexier than her lying there in nothing but her slip of a bra, with everything else bared to his eyes?

"Turn over," Carter demanded. Lorraine eyed him curiously, cautiously. "You can trust me," he assured her.

Her expression clearly said that she wasn't sure she could trust him, but she followed his orders all the same. She turned over and stretched out on her stomach. Her pert butt was too perfect for him not to go straight for it, but Carter resisted.

Instead, he started with her feet, massaging the arch of one and then the other with the pads of his thumbs. He worked his way up the backs of her legs, kneading her calf muscles, the backs of her thighs, that firm backside. He rubbed the small of her back with circular strokes, then slid his fingers up farther. He arrived at the single-clasp closure of her bra and unhooked it, letting the material fall, but leaving it on her arms.

"God, you're sexy," Carter breathed against her skin as he leaned over to place a kiss at the small of her back. He moved lower, nipping at her backside with gentle bites. Then he zeroed in on that spot between her legs again. Using his thumbs, he spread her open and fitted his tongue inside the delicate pink flesh.

Lorraine gasped. Then sighed. Her sexy moans were like a siren's call, encouraging him to go on and on. He couldn't get enough of the taste of her.

"Carter," Lorraine said with a sigh. "I need you inside me." She gasped. "Please."

That was all he needed to hear.

Reaching for the condom he'd slipped in his pocket earlier, Carter stood up, unzipped his jeans and pushed them down.

Lorraine started to turn, but he stopped her.

"No," Carter said. "Stay just the way you are."

She peered at him over her shoulder, her eyes heavy with desire. Carter quickly rolled the condom over his erection and dropped to the dais again. He knelt between Lorraine's legs, slipped an arm under her stomach and lifted her lower half off the floor. Then he fitted himself into her opening and entered her from behind.

Damn. She was just as tight as she'd been last night,

and it felt even better in this position. Carter moved in and out of her, one hand cradling her flat belly, the other on her hip, guiding her as her body bumped up against his. He loved the feel of her moist skin against him, how it slicked back and forth against his thighs, how it surrounded his cock. His body was hyperaware of every single part of her that touched him.

Carter had known that as soon as he got inside her, it wouldn't be long before his body erupted. He tried to hold off for as long as possible, but the need was too great. Either he gave in to his body's demands or his head would explode.

He could only get in three more good thrusts before he came, his arms trembling as he tried to keep his hold of Lorraine.

His knees buckled and he fell onto her back, but quickly rolled over so that he wouldn't crush her. He lolled his head to the side and found Lorraine staring at him through slitted eyes, still on her stomach.

"Are you falling asleep?" he asked her.

"Possibly," she answered dreamily. "I could use a nice long nap."

They both lay prone on the floor, completely naked. After a few minutes, Carter rolled to his side and scooped Lorraine up against him.

"You know, there is a bed," she said. She gestured to the left corner of the vast loft. "It's behind that half wall over there."

"So why did we do this on the floor?"

"Because the bed was just too damn far."

Carter laughed up at the ceiling. "Such language, Lorraine Elise. What would your mother say?"

"I doubt my language would be the thing to raise my mother's eyebrows."

"She would have a heart attack if she were to walk through that door, wouldn't she?"

"Don't worry. There is no chance of that happening. Trina is the only person in my family who knows about this place."

Carter frowned. "Why?"

She affected a snooty, nasally voice. "Because Hawthorne-Hayeses are jewelers, not artists." Her laugh was hollow.

"So your parents don't know that their sweet little innocent Lorraine is the infamous L. Elise?"

"No," she said quietly. "They have only seen a few of my paintings, and certainly not any of my erotic art." She turned around so she could face him. "At one time, it devastated me that my parents would not support something that is so dear to my heart, but not anymore. I've received enough feedback from people whose opinions I trust to know that I'm talented."

"You're more than just talented. Your work is fabulous."

She smiled. "Thank you, but the fact that your naked body is huddled against mine makes you a tad biased."

"I loved L. Elise's paintings way before I knew she and the woman I'm doing the nasty with were one and the same."

She gasped, and slapped his arm. "Doing the nasty? How very eighteen-year-old-frat-boy of you, Carter."

He laughed at her indignation, and marveled at how she could pull it off while she lay naked in his arms. Miss Prim and Proper could turn on the haughty socialite like a faucet.

"I gave up being a frat boy a long time ago," Carter said.

"So you belong to a fraternity?"

He nodded. "I joined it because my father and uncle belonged to the same fraternity and I wanted to fit it, but it wasn't for me."

"That's just as well. I'm not a fan of frat boys."

"Now, I've got a question for you." He pushed back a lock of hair that had fallen against her cheek. "If it doesn't matter whether or not your family approves, why do you still hide this place from them?"

"Because it's mine. This is my sanctuary. I can be myself—lose myself—when I'm here."

"I think I understand," he said, pulling her even more closely against him. "That's the way I feel when I'm baking. I have my particular spot at Lillian's, and everyone knows not to be there when it's time for me to bake. I sometimes wonder if I will ever be able to bake anywhere else."

"You mean during the *You Take the Cake* competition? Are you afraid you won't be comfortable baking on a Hollywood set?"

"No, I mean when I leave Lillian's."

Her brow furrowed. "Are you thinking of leaving?"

Carter debated for a moment whether he should say anything more, but as he looked around the loft, he realized that Lorraine had trusted him with this very private, personal part of herself. He should be able to do the same.

"I've been talking to a restaurateur in New York. He's offered me an executive pastry chef position with his organization."

Her eyes widened in surprise. "What does your family have to say about this?"

"They don't know. The only person I've told is my best friend, Malik."

She was quiet for several moments. "This is a big

step. Although I must be honest, Carter—I don't understand why you would be interested. Lillian's has such
an outstanding reputation in Chicago. It seems as if you
are already at the height of your profession. Why would
you need to seek something else?"

"Because I don't fit in at Lillian's." He grimaced, hating the whine he heard in his voice, but Carter knew this
was at the crux of his issues with the bakery. With everything. "I'm tired of feeling like an outsider. It doesn't
matter how many write-ups my cakes get in *Chicago
Today,* or the *Tribune* or on online blogs. It just never
feels as if I'm doing enough. I'm always going to be the
bastard grandson who should feel grateful that he's even
been given a place at the table."

"Oh, Carter." Her hand came up to caress his jaw.

He hated seeing the pity in her eyes and, in the same
breath, was touched by it. She actually cared about his
feelings, cared how his world was affected. Had he ever
felt this kind of empathy from someone? This kind of…
love?

Was this love?

He ran his hand down the side of her cheek. "I'm
falling really hard for you, Rainey. It scares the crap
out of me."

A sad smile tilted her lips. "I know the feeling," she
said. "I'm falling just as hard." Her piercing eyes seared
him. "Please be real, Carter."

"What do you mean by that?"

"Don't be some mirage that looks so genuine on the
outside, but turns into something different when I get
too close."

"I'm one hundred percent real," he said. He leaned in,
his lips hovering mere inches from her mouth. "That's
a promise."

Chapter 10

Lorraine stood before the small college-dorm-size refrigerator in a T-shirt and bare feet. She hadn't bothered with underwear. Carter told her it would just hinder access.

"I only have diet soda and water," she called.

"Diet soda kills," Carter called back.

Lorraine chuckled and grabbed two bottles of water. She walked over to where he stood in front of some of her less risqué portraits. He looked like pure sin standing there with his chest and feet both bare, his jeans riding low on his hips. The jeans were unbuckled and partially unzipped, for the same reason she was going sans panties and bra.

She handed him the bottle of water. "Diet soda does not kill."

"It kills taste buds." He took the water from her and placed a kiss on the tip of her nose, then motioned to the paintings. "The only L. Elise paintings I've seen are the naked—" She gave him a stern look. "The more erotic ones," he corrected. "But these are spectacular. Have you had showings of your…what should I call them… normal paintings?"

"I've only offered a few to galleries. The L. Elise name has become synonymous with sensual art. I'm unsure if people will accept, to quote you, 'normal' paintings from L. Elise."

"Maybe you should put them out under your real name," he suggested.

Lorraine huffed out a humorless laugh. "I can only imagine my parents' reaction." She couldn't keep the sarcasm from her voice, though she didn't really try to.

"Why do you even care what they think? You have an amazing talent, and you're keeping it hidden because you don't want to upset your parents? That's crazy."

"It is so much more complicated than you can possibly comprehend," she said.

He crossed his arms over his chest. "Try me."

She shook her head. "It doesn't matter. These paintings are more for my enjoyment. I'm not ready to share them yet."

But that was a lie. She was more than ready for the world to know that Lorraine Hawthorne-Hayes was good for more than just attending society functions. She was ready for the world to see the talent she possessed. It was the reason she'd applied for that fellowship, the reason she'd begun painting less provocative subjects that would be more acceptable in galleries around the city.

Carter stared at her for several long moments, looking as if he wanted to say more, but blessedly, he let the subject drop. He continued his stroll, observing the numerous paintings taking up nearly every inch of space along the walls of the loft. He came upon the one painting she usually avoided. It was a self-portrait of her looking out of a window, with streams of rains rolling down the glass.

He set his water bottle on the floor and picked up the canvas. "What's this one called?" he asked.

She took a deep breath before answering. *"Just Lorraine."*

He flashed her a surprised look. "The real name, huh? So, I'm guessing it's not going into anyone's gallery."

"No," she said. "This one is just for me. I painted it about five years ago."

He pointed to the canvas. "Are these raindrops or tears?"

She cocked her head to the side and stared at the painting along with him. "It's up to the observer to decide."

Carter studied the painting for a few moments longer, then carefully set it against the wall with the others. He turned to her, and said, "I think they're tears."

Lorraine hunched her shoulders, her throat clogged with too much emotion to speak.

Carter took a step closer. He trailed a single finger down her cheek. "What could have brought you so much sadness?"

Lorraine leaned into his touch. "Please, don't ask me that," she said. "It still hurts too much to talk about."

"Tell me." His softly whispered plea tore at her heart. He hooked that lone finger underneath her chin and lifted her face to meet his gaze. "Tell me, Rainey. What happened to you? What broke your spirit?"

Lorraine shut her eyes against the tears that instantly formed, but two still managed to escape. Her skin tingled at the feel of Carter's thumbs wiping the moisture from her cheeks. She opened her eyes, studying his face through the blur of tears.

"I made a stupid mistake," she said.

"Who hasn't?" he asked softly.

A sad smile pulled at her lips. "Most people's mistakes don't cost them a million dollars."

Carter pulled in a swift breath as his head snapped back. "What happened?"

Lorraine took a couple of steps back and wrapped her arms around her upper body. She couldn't look at him while sharing her most embarrassing secret.

"It was my junior year of college. I had been dating my boyfriend for about four months, almost five. Of course, I thought I was in love." She swiped at her cheeks again. "When he asked me to pose for some pictures, I was all too happy to oblige. He was going to Europe to study international finance for a semester, and told me he needed something to keep him warm on those cold, lonely nights."

Lorraine heard Carter's curse.

"I'm sure you've guessed what happened next."

"He blackmailed you," he said.

She shook her head. "Not me. The first time I actually saw the pictures with my own eyes was when my father showed them to me." Her voice was barely a whisper when she said, "It's not the father/daughter moment most people dream about."

"Oh, God." Carter came up to her and wrapped his arms around her.

Lorraine glommed onto the comfort his embrace provided. "My father paid him one million dollars to destroy the pictures."

"And you think he actually did? You don't think he

has copies stored on a computer somewhere? What's to stop the bastard from coming after more money?"

"That's the one thing I'm afraid of."

"Why didn't your dad just go to the police?"

"Because the story would have gotten out," Lorraine said. "It would have been just as detrimental as if the actual pictures had been released."

Carter wrapped his arms tighter around her. "I'm so sorry."

"No one else in my family other than me and my parents know about this. Not even Trina or Stuart. I can't imagine the humiliation I would have faced had my father not paid him. It would have tarnished the entire Hawthorne-Hayes Jewelry name. Who would want to buy their engagement ring or Mother's Day pendant from a jeweler attached to a sex scandal?"

"You were a young college kid who'd been duped by an unscrupulous asshole. You can't keep beating yourself up over it."

"How can I not? It would have been detrimental, Carter. I take full blame for this. I'm the one who let him take those pictures of me." She shook her head. "I came so close to causing irreparable damage to everything my father worked so hard to build. I owe both him and my mother so much. Without their help, my ex-boyfriend would have ruined me."

She pulled in a deep, shuddering breath.

"That is why I vowed to be the dutiful daughter and live up to my grandmother's name. That is why L. Elise must remain a secret."

"Why can't there be room for both?" Carter asked. "What's stopping you from sharing your paintings and being the epitome of what an upstanding Hawthorne-Hayes is supposed to be?" He lifted her chin and stared into her eyes. "Your art is who you are, Lorraine. You can't continue to hide it."

"I know," she said. "I just have to figure out how to meld the two halves of myself. I fear if I don't do something more with my art, I'm going to slowly die inside."

"I won't allow that to happen," Carter said. "Do you know that this has been the most excited I've ever seen you, when you were showing me your paintings? You're happier when you're surrounded by your art. Don't you want to feel this way all the time, Rainey?"

She nodded as another tear escaped.

"Then go for it. This is your true self. You have to stop hiding it from the world."

Lorraine slipped her hand up to his jaw and cradled it in her palm.

"You are very good for me, Carter Drayson." Her voice fell to a whisper. "I think I'm falling in love with you."

His heated look seared her. "I think I've already fallen."

"This is crazy," she said. "Love doesn't happen this quickly, Carter."

"It has never happened at all for me," he said. "I wasn't running some kind of game on you when I said I've never felt this way, Lorraine. But I don't know what other word I could use to describe it. This has to be love."

Then he leaned in close and captured her lips in a slow, easy kiss that was unlike anything she could ever make up in her vivid imagination.

The next morning, Carter drove Lorraine home and parked her car in her designated parking space. He was preparing to walk her up to her door, but he was already running late, and Lorraine assured him it was unnecessary. He walked the few blocks from her Gold Coast high-rise to Lillian's, grateful for the change of clothes he kept tucked in a backpack in one of the consultation offices.

This wasn't his first time having to go straight to the bakery after being out all night, although it was usually after a night of hard partying and no sleep. He hadn't had much sleep last night, but those few hours that he'd spooned against Lorraine, his arms wrapped around her soft, petite frame, were some of the best hours of sleep he'd ever had.

He'd told her he loved her last night.

Instant panic seized his chest. Carter tried to tamp it down. It was ridiculous that just the thought of falling in love could evoke such terror, but it was there, clawing at his throat, making it hard to breathe.

He didn't do love, especially this intense, all-consuming kind he was starting to feel for Lorraine. That kind of love existed for his grandmother's generation, and maybe a few others here and there, but it just wasn't in the cards for him.

Look at his own parents. There sure as hell wasn't any love lost there.

What if in the middle of all of this he pulled a Devon Drayson and decided that the love and marriage thing just wasn't for him?

Wait. *Marriage?* Who was talking marriage?

"Stop thinking so damn much." Carter cursed underneath his breath. They had only been dating for a few weeks. He needed to chill the hell out and stop creating problems where none existed. He and Lorraine enjoyed each other's company. He was having more fun with her than with any woman he'd ever been with before. Why couldn't he just enjoy it and stop thinking so damn much?

Carter entered through the back door at Lillian's and immediately noticed a marked uptick in the usual noise level. Drake came out of one of the offices and pointed at Carter.

"Is that what you're wearing?" his cousin asked.

"Wearing for what?"

"Didn't you get Shari's text message? There's a local news crew in the bakery. They're doing a feature on Lillian's participation in *You Take the Cake*."

Carter had left his phone charger at home when he and Lorraine had left for her loft, not realizing that he wouldn't be returning to his apartment. His phone had died sometime during the night, so any text messages were waiting in limbo land.

"Come on, man," Drake said. "You know they're going to want to interview you after all the press the animal cakes got after the Lincoln Park Zoo event."

Carter looked down at his rumpled T-shirt and jeans. He thought the only thing he would be doing today was meeting with Drake and Malik about the upcoming book. He'd had no plans to even go into the retail portion of the bakery.

"Keep them occupied for a few minutes while I change," Carter told his cousin. He quickly made it to the consultation office and pulled out the backpack he kept in the bottom drawer of the filing cabinet. The polo shirt he pulled out was almost as wrinkled as his T-shirt, but at least it had a collar. Carter slipped into the bathroom with his toiletry bag and a couple of minutes later, made his way into the storefront where the TV crew was interviewing Shari in front of a display of Lillian's prepackaged brownie mixes.

"And here is the man behind those fabulous cakes that were on display at the Comer Children's Hospital 'View the Zoo' event at Lincoln Park Zoo," the reporter said, stepping over to Carter.

Carter dialed up his most charming smile and answered her questions regarding what went into making such elaborate cakes.

"Lillian's has always been a favorite here in Chicago, but your cakes in particular are becoming just as renowned, Carter. How does it feel?"

"It feels wonderful to know that people are enjoying my creations," he answered. "I work hard at my craft, and it's great to hear that customers appreciate my hard work."

"All of Chicago is looking forward to cheering you on in the *You Take the Cake* competition next month." The reporter turned to the camera. "The great thing about this story is that the desserts taste just as fabulous as they look." She took a bite out of a chocolate petit four. "Back to you, John."

Carter turned, and found Drake standing less than a foot away. "*My* creations? Way to be a team player, Carter. Maybe you should just go out there to California by yourself. You don't need the rest of us."

"Don't be an asshole," Carter spat. "You know that's not how I meant it."

"Really? It sounded that way."

"Just because you're insecure about your place in the business, don't take it out on me," Carter said, instantly recognizing the irony in that statement. If anyone was insecure about his worth to Lillian's, it was him.

Drake pointed toward the camera crew, who were wrapping up their equipment. "You know who got them to come here? I did. They followed a link I tweeted to

Lillian's Facebook page and contacted me there. So I know exactly what I do for this bakery."

Carter wasn't up for this discussion today—or ever. "Look, are we discussing the *Brothers Who Bake* cookbook this morning, or what? If not, I've got other things I can be doing on my day off."

"You do realize that Grandma Lillian and Grandpa Henry's decision of who will run the bakery will depend on more than just who bakes the best, right?"

"Are we talking about *Brothers Who Bake?*" Carter repeated.

Drake's lips thinned into a sharp line, but he didn't press any more. "Malik is in the kitchen."

"Then let's get this over with." The quicker he finished here at Lillian's, the quicker he could take time to think about just what was happening between him and Lorraine. He'd never told a woman that he loved her before and actually *meant* it. He needed to figure out if he meant it this time.

Although Carter had a feeling he already knew the answer to that question.

Chapter 11

Lorraine turned off the shower and stepped onto the plush bathroom rug. It had felt almost as if she'd traveled ten years back in time when she'd slipped into the penthouse an hour ago, like a risky fifteen-year-old crossing her fingers that no one would hear her sneaking in. Thankfully, her parents either were still lingering in their wing of the apartment or, hopefully, had left altogether. They were due for a quick trip to France or Morocco any day now.

She wrapped her hair in a towel and pulled her silk robe from the hook behind her bathroom door. She slipped into it, her mind set on draping herself across the bed and sleeping for a few hours before she actually did something productive today. That is, *if* she could find something productive to do today. Something more than answering correspondence from one of the society groups her mother had forced her to join.

Lorraine stepped out of her bathroom and stopped short.

Her mother stood in the middle of her bedroom, holding a brown manila folder.

"What are you doing in my room?" Lorraine asked, tightening the belt on her robe.

"Did you have a good time with your baker friend last night?" her mother asked.

"His name is Carter," Lorraine bit out between clenched teeth.

"Yes, I know." Her mother opened the folder and peered at the pages inside. "Carter Drayson. Son of Devon Drayson, the youngest, *bachelor* son of Lillian and Henry Drayson," her mother continued. "Carter's mother and father were never married."

"I know that," Lorraine said. "What is your point, Mother?"

"Carter never finished college. He dropped out after his freshman year."

"He went to culinary school. In fact, he attended one of the best culinary schools in the country. Again, what is your point, Mother?"

"My point is that I do not approve of my daughter dating a college dropout with a reputation that is equivalent to that of a male whore."

Lorraine flinched at her harsh words. "You don't know what you're talking about."

Her mother held up the folder. "It's right here in black and white. The private investigator I hired uncovered several interesting things about your baker."

"You had Carter investigated?" Lorraine asked with disbelief.

"Yes, I did," her mother hissed.

"You had no right."

"I had *every* right!" her mother said with an uncharacteristic shout. "Or have you forgotten just what it cost this family the last time you fell head over heels for some smooth talker, Lorraine?"

"Carter and Broderick are nothing alike," Lorraine defended. "Don't you dare put them in the same category."

"Carter Drayson and Broderick Collins are more alike than you know. Do you remember when you discovered that Broderick was seeing at least a half dozen other women?"

Lorraine's stomach felt as if it were filled with lead. "Carter isn't seeing anyone else," she said.

"I couldn't find proof that he's seeing someone else now, but do you have any idea how many women he has been linked to in the past?"

"Probably as many as your own son," Lorraine countered. "Do you think Stuart is some eunuch that spends all of his time in the jewelry store? Please, Mother."

"I have no illusions about what Stuart does, but your brother is discreet. He knows how to conduct himself, and every single girl he has ever dated comes from good breeding."

"Carter is a Drayson!" Lorraine practically screeched.

"He is also a playboy who collects women the way I collect shoes. You don't know anything about this man, but it's all here." Her mother tossed the folder onto her bed. "Why don't you read it? Then see if you feel the same way about your little baker once you consider just how many women came before you."

Lorraine crossed her arms over her chest. "I don't need to read a report on Carter. If I have any questions, I can go straight to the source."

"Do you think he would tell you the truth?"

"What would that report tell me?"

"It would tell you that in all of his thirty years, Carter Drayson has dated dozens of women, but has never been seriously linked to a single one of them. Not one, Lorraine. Yet, all of a sudden, he only has eyes for you?"

"Is that so hard to believe?"

"When you've only been dating for a few weeks? Yes, that is hard for me to believe. Do you really think this man has fallen head over heels for you, Lorraine? Do you think that's what his eyes are really focused on? He may be a Drayson, but that is nothing compared to being a Hawthorne-Hayes. And there are quite a few Drayson grandchildren. That money pot would have to be split among a fair amount of people."

"Oh, my God, Mother. Not everyone thinks the way you do. Carter does not want me for my money."

"I'm sure you thought the same of Broderick Collins."

Lorraine flinched at her mother's well-placed barb. The woman knew exactly what to say to draw the most blood.

"You are not a good judge of character, Lorraine. Do not get caught up in all the flowers and romance. You need to take a good look at exactly who this Carter Drayson is, and think about what he really is after."

For several minutes after her mother had exited the room, Lorraine remained where she stood. She stared at the offending file folder lying on her sage-green satin comforter. She told herself to march to the bed, grab it and throw it in the trash—preferably in front of her mother's face.

But she couldn't do it.

And she hated herself for it.

She hated herself even more with every step she took

toward the bed. By the time she sank onto the plush mattress and pulled the folder onto her lap, her self-loathing was enough to smother her.

But she still opened the file.

Lorraine snuggled closer against Carter as the Ferris wheel took another huge loop. The air was brisk against her face, with just the slightest chill.

"The city looks so peaceful from here. It is breathtaking."

"Don't you have an even better view from over there?" he asked, pointing to her high-rise building in Gold Coast, which they could see from the Ferris wheel.

"It's not the same," Lorraine said. "I feel so free up here. As if I don't have a care in the world. It feels heavenly."

"And you weren't sure when I told you I was taking you to Navy Pier," Carter said as he placed a kiss against her temple.

"I told you that I had a horrible experience the last time I came here. As long as I stay away from the swings, I should be okay."

"That's where I had planned to take you next," he teased.

Lorraine pinched his arm and then held on tighter to it. She rested her head against his shoulder, trying to block out the things she'd read in the private investigator's report. It didn't matter how many women Carter had dated, or that none of his relationships seemed to last very long. She knew what she felt right now, and it was unlike anything she'd ever felt before. She was not going to let some P.I. her mother had hired mar her vision of Carter.

Their seat came to a stop at the base of the Ferris wheel and they got off.

"I promised you dinner," Carter said. "I guess it's time I make good on my promise."

Walking hand in hand, they bypassed the restaurants along the pier and headed for the food court. Lorraine laughed at Carter's shocked look when she admitted that she did not like the traditional Chicago-style hot dog.

"I'm sorry," she said. "I'm not a fan of tomatoes, or those seeded buns."

"Next thing you'll tell me is that you root for the Cubs instead of the White Sox."

Lorraine scrunched up her nose. "Is that football or basketball?"

Carter's head fell forward with his weary sigh.

"I'm just kidding." She laughed. "I know that the White Sox is a baseball team, but you would never catch me watching a game, no matter who is playing."

Carter purchased two hot dogs—a traditional Chicago dog for himself and a plain frank on a bun for her—then guided her to a less-crowded area on the pier. They stood against the railing, eating their hot dogs. Just then, something sailed past them, making a plopping sound as it hit the water.

A voice yelled, "Come here, Ethan!" and a young boy came running up to the railing. Carter caught him just in time.

"Whoa, there," he said, catching the toddler by the waist.

The little boy pointed at the inky water and said, "Truck."

"Ethan!" The father came up to the railing, pushing a stroller with a baby who couldn't be more than a few months old. The man was puffing like someone who'd just run a marathon. "Ethan, never run away like that again," the father scolded. He turned to Carter. "Thank you."

"You're welcome," Carter said. "But I think you'll need to buy a new T.R.U.C.K." He pointed to the water.

Thanking Carter again, the father attached one of those kid leashes to the curly redhead's tiny wrist and continued on.

"Looks as if he's got his hands full," Carter said.

"I give him kudos for being brave enough to bring such young kids out to the pier, but I do hope the mother is in the restroom or something. I'm not sure he will make it much longer on his own."

Carter laughed. "Dad looked as if he was ready to dive in that water just to get away." He looked over at her, his head tilted slightly. In a softer, muted tone, he asked, "Do you want kids?"

"Yes," she answered without hesitation. She dreamed of having children someday. And actually being there for them instead of allowing a nanny or housekeeper to raise them. "What about you?"

He shrugged. "I haven't thought about it all that much. Kids are so much responsibility."

"Does that scare you?"

"In a way, yeah. When I do have kids, I want to do it right."

"What do you mean by that?"

He was silent for so long that Lorraine wondered if he would continue. "I don't want this to come out the wrong way, because I do love both of my parents, and I know my mom tried her hardest to do right by me, but I've always resented the fact that they were never married. They're the reason I stood out, the reason I'm different from my cousins."

"What makes you so sure things would have been better for you if they had been married?" she asked him.

"Oh, I know better than to think that," Carter said with a humorless laugh. "As much as I resented the fact that they didn't get married, I know it would have been a disaster. They've never gotten along. It makes me wonder how they tolerated each other long enough to actually make me." He turned around and leaned back against the railing. "But in all these years, neither of them ever came close to marrying anyone else, either. It makes me wonder if I'm even wired for marriage."

Lorraine was silent for a long stretch of time. It wasn't as if she had been hoping for a marriage proposal. She and Carter had only been dating for a few weeks. But the way he was talking right now, it felt as if he didn't think he would ever be marriage material.

It broke her heart that he saw himself as someone who wasn't worthy enough for the kind of love that came with marriage. That wasn't the Carter Drayson she saw when she looked at him. She saw a man who placed her feelings—her pleasure—above his own. The man she saw standing next to her was selfless and so full of love that he took her breath away. Why could he not see the same?

"I think they may put us off the pier if we continue with this conversation much longer," Carter said. "Our mopey frowns will run the guests off."

Lorraine laughed, loving the way he could so effortlessly put a smile on her face.

Carter announced that he had room for dessert, so he went in search of ice cream. Leaning against the railing that lined the pier, Lorraine looked out over the water, her mind once again drifting to that private investigator's report and all the women it had listed as being a part of Carter's past.

She was no psychologist, but after their previous conversation, she couldn't help thinking that Carter's association with all those women had something to do with how he saw his parents' relationship. Maybe, without even knowing it, he had created a self-fulfilling prophecy by not giving himself the chance to develop a long, stable relationship.

She was not going to allow that to happen to them. Carter had come to mean too much to her in these few short weeks. She'd never felt so alive, so full of life. She wasn't ready to give him up.

"I hope you like mint chocolate chip."

She turned to find Carter holding two ice-cream cones and a white bag.

"I've got ice cream and Garrett's caramel corn. It's dessert heaven."

"Or a ticket to the gym," Lorraine said, taking the ice-cream cone from him.

"You don't need a gym." Carter pressed a kiss to her temple. In a decidedly sexy voice, he whispered, "I've got my own workout regimen for you."

"You can't help being naughty, can you?" She laughed.

"Not when I'm around you," he admitted. "Are you ready for the concert?"

With a nod, she grabbed on to his hand that held the bag of popcorn and they headed toward the stage area, where a local band Trina had mentioned was scheduled to hold a live concert. As they walked hand in hand, a group of three women who looked to be about her age walked toward them. They didn't try to hide their ogling as they looked Carter up and down. Carter seemed oblivious, but Lorraine certainly was not.

She begged herself to just let it go, but she couldn't hold back, not with the things she'd read in that P.I. report still fresh in her mind.

"So," Lorraine said, trying to keep her tone as playful as possible, "just how many women have been treated to the Carter Drayson Experience?"

He looked over at her. "The Carter Drayson Experience?"

"You must know what I'm asking, Carter. I'm not naive. I know I'm not the first."

"I told you from the beginning that I haven't been a choirboy," he said.

"I'm not judging you." Yes, she was. "I just want to know. Am I the twenty-first? Fifty-first?"

"Rainey, I haven't kept count."

"So, there have been enough that you'd lose count?" *Just shut up,* Lorraine pleaded with herself.

Carter stopped walking and turned to her. "Where is all of this coming from?"

It was on the tip of her tongue to tell him about the P.I. report, but she could only imagine what Carter would think. Any negative reaction would be completely warranted. How could she even begin to explain her mother's actions to him?

Instead, Lorraine decided to take another approach. It was a partial truth.

"Even though you seem oblivious of it, there have been quite a few women checking you out, Carter."

A smile crept up the sides of his mouth. "Are you jealous?"

Lorraine frowned at him, giving him the evil eye. "Maybe a little," she admitted.

Carter pitched what was left of his ice-cream cone in a nearby trash bin and turned to her. He lifted her chin up to his gaze. "You have absolutely nothing to worry about," he said. "I'll be the first to admit that I'm not a saint. I've done some things in the past that I'm not proud of, and when I think about it now, I wonder how I could have been so…indiscriminate, for lack of a better word."

"How indiscriminate?"

"Are you really going to judge me based on my past?"

"I don't want to," she said.

"If I'd known that someone like you was on the horizon, I would have made very different choices," he said.

Her skin instantly flushed with the most delicious warmth.

"I'm not the man I was a month ago, Rainey. You've changed me in so many ways. It scared the hell out of me at first, but I realize that I like the man I am when I'm with you."

Lorraine brought her hand to her chest, afraid her heart would burst at his beautiful words.

"I'm sorry I ever doubted you," she said.

"That's okay," Carter said as he leaned in close, his lips hovering just a smidgen above hers. "I can think of a dozen ways that you can make it up to me."

Chapter 12

"You are going to get me into so much trouble," Lorraine whispered in his ear.

"How's that?" he asked, his voice equally soft.

"I was scheduled to attend a Junior League meeting this morning. Yet here I am, sneaking out to be with you."

"You could have said no when I called."

"You knew I couldn't resist this invitation," she said.

Carter tried to staunch the cagey smile playing at his lips. It was a good thing the room was dimly lit. Maybe she wouldn't see it.

"I know," he said, the words coming out with a hint of mischievousness, despite his best effort to hide it.

Lorraine pinched his arm as they strolled to the next exhibit.

When he'd extended an invitation to attend a special Marcel Duchamp exhibition being held at the Field Museum, Carter knew she wouldn't be able to resist. As he'd predicted, Lorraine blew off her schedule for the day. When he'd picked her up from her building, she'd admitted that it was the third time she'd cancelled on previously held commitments since she and Carter had begun dating.

Carter had experienced a stab of guilt, and had offered to take her to the exhibit another time, but Lorraine wouldn't hear of it.

"You've helped me to rediscover that fun, spontaneous side of myself that I'd buried after the incident with my ex-boyfriend," she'd told him. "I didn't realize just how much I miss being that girl."

He had to admit that he liked that girl, too.

Spotlights shone on the paintings and small sculptures encased in glass. As they viewed the paintings, Lorraine explained tidbits she'd learned about many of them while studying as an art history major. She'd been surprised by the fact that he knew several of her little-known facts.

"Did you know that Duchamp had a pseudonym? He was also known as Rose Selavy."

"A woman?"

She nodded. "He dressed in drag and had a series of photographs taken. They are on display at museums throughout the U.S. and Europe."

"Now, that I didn't know," Carter said. "What little-known fact will people say about you when they're looking at your work hanging in a museum?"

She lowered her voice even more than the whispered tones they were already using. "I doubt any of L. Elise's work would be welcome in the Field Museum," she said.

"Maybe not, but Lorraine Hawthorne-Hayes's would be," he said. "Maybe in the Hawthorne-Hayes gallery?

If I'm not mistaken, I do believe I saw one of those silver plaques with Arnold and Abigail Hawthorne-Hayes etched into it."

"You did," Lorraine answered. "My father supports the arts, but he still does not approve of his daughter being an artist." Her laugh was light, but Carter caught the hint of sadness. "It is ridiculously hypocritical, but it doesn't matter. As I've previously stated, those paintings that I paint under my own name are just for me."

Carter was stunned by the rush of frustration that swiftly tore through him. "Are you telling me that you plan to keep your talent hidden for the rest of your life? Do you really want people to think that all there is to Lorraine Hawthorne-Hayes is a rich socialite who throws afternoon teas?"

The flash of hurt that etched across her face caused his chest to tighten with remorse.

"That's not fair," she said, her voice muted.

Carter dialed back his tone. He caught her chin between his fingers and lifted her face up so that he could look into her eyes.

"No, it isn't," he said. "It's not fair to *you*. You have unbelievable talent. You need to take credit for it."

"I'm not one to brag about my work, Carter. It's not about that for me."

"There's a difference between bragging and owning what's rightfully yours, Rainey. This gift you've been given is amazing. *Own it.* I don't care how much you try to convince yourself that you're happy as the mysterious L. Elise. I know deep down you want people to know that Lorraine is the genius behind those paintings."

The glimmer of a smile played at the corners of her lips. "Well, perhaps a little," she admitted.

Carter joined her in her smile. "I knew it."

His phone let out a beep. He pulled it from his pocket to silence it, then noticed the reminder that had popped up on the screen. "Oh, damn. How did I forget about this? We're going to have to cut this short," he said. "I have a standing date at the University of Chicago Medicine's pediatric burn unit. Do you mind?"

"Of course not," Lorraine said. "Can I join you?"

"Are you sure?"

She nodded.

They left the museum and headed back to Lillian's. As they were driving, Carter called the bakery and ordered three dozen cupcakes to be boxed up for him. Jason was waiting with the stacked boxes when they pulled into the alleyway behind Lillian's.

They drove south to the Hyde Park neighborhood where the hospital was located. Carter parked, but before he opened the car door he turned to her.

"This won't be easy," he warned. "The burns on some of these kids…" Carter pulled in a deep breath. "The first time I came here, I almost left halfway through my visit. I'm talking second- and third-degree burns over sixty percent of their bodies. Some of them have been in here for months. It's amazing the progress that's been made."

"You do this often?" she asked.

"At least once a month," he answered. "These kids don't even get the chance to attend events like the one at Lincoln Park Zoo the other night because of the risk of infection. And it's actually easier to bring cookies, cupcakes or brownies to the kids in the burn unit. You never know what kind of restrictive diets the kids in the other wards are on, and if you think seeing a sick kid lying in a hospital bed is hard, just wait until you see that same kid after you're forced to tell him that he can't have a cupcake."

Lorraine put her hand to her chest. "I'm sure it's heartbreaking."

Carter nodded. "So, you think you're up for this?"

"Absolutely." She nodded.

A grin broke out across his face. Carter trailed a finger down her cheek. "You've got yourself a pretty good con going here," he said.

Her brow dipped in an affronted frown. "What do you mean by that?"

"You pretend to be this delicate little flower on the outside, but you, Lorraine Hawthorne-Hayes, are what my grandmother would call a steel magnolia." Carter leaned across the seat and placed a kiss on her nose. "Come on, let's go brighten the day of a few kids."

Lorraine braced herself for the worst as she followed Carter into the burn unit, but despite some of the truly horrific burns and disfigured faces, all she could see was joy. As she and Carter made their way from bed to bed, delivering cupcakes, the children's eyes lit up with delight.

The way Carter interacted with the children was something Lorraine knew she would remember for years to come. He possessed such a gentle, generous soul. It melted her heart every time he smiled at the kids, or playfully put a dollop of frosting on one's nose.

They entered the room of a little girl who looked to be about ten years old. She was sitting up in bed, and appeared as normal as any other little girl, with no visible burns.

Carter knocked on the Plexiglas wall. "Is anybody home?"

"Hi, Carter," she answered.

"I saved the best for last," Carter said. "Rainey, this is Delaney. Delaney, my friend Rainey. You two almost have the same name."

"Hi, Rainey," she said, her smile bright as the sun.

"Hello there," Lorraine answered. "How are you?"

"Good. I'll be better with a cupcake," she said, and Lorraine burst out laughing. She opened the box and held it out to her. "Which do you want, chocolate or vanilla?"

The little girl looked to Carter.

"Uh, I usually don't make Delaney pick. She gets two," he said, and the little girl excitedly picked up two cupcakes.

Lorraine sent him a curious look, but he surreptitiously shook his head. She glanced around the room, and noticed a series of drawings tacked to the walls.

"Did you draw these?" she asked Delaney. The little girl nodded as she licked icing from her knuckle. "They are very good," Lorraine commented.

"Thank you," Delaney said around a mouthful of cupcake.

Lorraine peered more closely at the incredibly detailed pencil sketches of birds, trees and whales. Her form was practically flawless.

"Delaney is quite the artist," Carter said. "She wants to draw real cartoons when she grows up, not the computer ones, right?"

The little girl nodded.

"Have you ever taken an art class?" Lorraine asked as she continued to study the sketches.

"No, but I didn't trace those," Delaney was quick to defend. "I drew them myself."

"Oh, I believe you. I used to do pencil sketches such

as these when I was in school. I would get in trouble, because I usually drew them during math class."

Delaney scrunched up her face. "I hate math."

"I know the feeling." Lorraine grinned in agreement.

"Hello, hello, hello." A woman dressed in pink scrubs entered the room, pushing a wheelchair. "It's time for someone's therapy."

Delaney's face scrunched up in the same way it had when she'd spoken of her dislike of math. "Can I finish my cupcake first?" she asked.

The nurse nodded, and Delaney took a mouse-size nibble of the cupcake she had been scarfing down just a moment ago.

"Don't try that trick," the nurse said. "You've got one minute to finish that cupcake."

The little girl frowned and stuffed the rest of the cupcake into her mouth. A moment later, the nurse removed the sheet covering Delaney's bottom half. Lorraine let out a gasp. The little girl's legs were so scarred and mangled, they were almost unrecognizable as human limbs. It was unlike anything Lorraine had ever seen.

"It's okay," Delaney said. "It doesn't hurt anymore."

"I'm so sorry," Lorraine said, feeling horribly insensitive. "I didn't mean anything by it."

"It's okay." Carter repeated Delaney's words. "We're used to it. And Delaney here is going to be okay. Those legs will be good as new soon, right?"

She gave Carter a thumbs-up.

"I'll see you next month," Carter told her.

"Bring the peanut butter and chocolate cupcakes next time," she told him before she was wheeled out of the room.

As soon as she was gone, Lorraine dropped into the

room's lone chair and cradled her face in her hands. "I feel like an idiot."

"Don't beat yourself up about that," Carter said. "I reacted the same way the first time I saw her burns. Unfortunately, Delaney is used to it."

"That doesn't make me feel any better, Carter." She fitted her fist against her lips. "That poor baby. What happened to her? Do you know?"

"Car fire," Carter said. "Her legs were pinned. Those burns actually go halfway up her torso, though it was her lower half that got the worst of it. She's had over twenty-five surgeries so far."

"Oh, my God," Lorraine gasped. She could not imagine what that poor child had endured.

"That's not the hardest part," Carter continued. "She lost both parents and her baby brother in the accident."

"My goodness! How is she even functioning?"

Carter shrugged. "You know what they say—kids are resilient. Her doctors think that her drawing has been a good escape for her."

"She's remarkably talented, but honestly, Carter, how does she do it? I would be in a catatonic state for the rest of my life if I'd gone through such a horrific experience."

"She's a tough kid, and she knows she can get anything she wants from me. I'll be back with peanut butter and chocolate cupcakes later today."

"Is she going into foster care when she's released from the hospital?" Lorraine asked, afraid to hear the answer. She could only imagine how scary this all must be for that sweet little girl.

"Her aunt and uncle have already been granted custody of her. They've all got a long road ahead of them, but they're grateful for what they have. That accident could have had zero survivors."

Lorraine remained in the chair, trying to wrap her brain around all that she'd learned in the past few minutes. She felt even more like a selfish, whiny brat for complaining these past few months over the state of her own life. Seeing these children today, realizing all they had had to endure in their short little lives already, humbled her beyond understanding.

"Are you ready?" Carter asked softly.

Lorraine nodded, unable to speak past the lump in her throat. She stopped in the doorway of Delaney's room one last time, looking around at the stuffed animals and pink bedding. Someone, probably her aunt, had tried to make the room look as much like a little girl's room as possible. She glanced once again at the pencil sketches on the walls, still blown away by the little girl's talent.

"Come on," Carter urged.

As he drove away from the hospital, Carter tried to engage her in conversation, but Lorraine wasn't in a talkative mood. She couldn't get Delaney, or any of the other children, out of her head. Some of them had been in that burn unit for months, enduring painful skin grafts and physical therapy, showing more strength than she'd had to summon in her entire life.

Seeing the way they faced their struggles with determination, some even with smiles on their faces, forced her to view her life through a different perspective.

They ended up at Carter's apartment, snuggled together on his sofa, watching television. It had quickly become Lorraine's favorite pastime, but tonight, she didn't find as much joy in the sitcom they watched. Her mind was still too consumed by what she'd witnessed today. Not only could she not get the children out of her mind, but she kept seeing Carter interacting with them. It played like a movie reel in her mind.

A reality that was hard to swallow settled into Lorraine's bones: her contribution to the world amounted to absolutely nothing. The truth sat like a weighty anchor in the pit of her stomach. She had always been taught that if there was ever a problem, just throw money at it. Problem solved.

But money meant very little to a young child confined to a bed, with more than half of her body burned. Those children didn't need money; they needed care. They needed compassion. Sometimes they needed something as simple as a cupcake.

She wanted—no, she *needed*—to find a way to give back. She needed to find something more meaningful. Something that had nothing to do with throwing Hawthorne-Hayes money around.

"What's up with you tonight?" Carter asked, pulling her closer to his side. "You're too quiet."

"I'm fine," she said. "I'm just enjoying your company."

He kissed the top of her head. "Thanks for coming with me to the hospital today."

"Thank you for bringing me. It was…" She pulled in a deep breath. "Eye-opening."

"It was hard," Carter said. "It always is, no matter how many times I go."

"It was, but my discomfort was nothing compared to what those kids go through." She peered up at Carter from where she lay against his chest. "I know I've told you this before, but you need to hear it again. You are a good man, Carter Drayson. Don't let anyone ever tell you differently."

"And you are a remarkable, talented woman, Lorraine Hawthorne-Hayes. Remember that." He kissed her lips. "And did I mention sexy?"

She laughed.

Lorraine settled back into the comfortable warmth his embrace created, wondering how she could ever have let her mother and that private investigator plant doubts into her head. It mattered not what Carter had done in the past. All that mattered was that the man she was with right now was one of the most loving, generous human beings she had ever encountered. That was enough for her.

Chapter 13

Carter propped himself upon a stool at the kitchen island, arms braced apart, eyes focused on his now silent cell phone. He'd been anticipating the phone conversation he'd just had for weeks, but never in a million years did he think he'd feel this way afterward.

He'd just received the official offer to become the executive pastry chef for Robinson Restaurants Group's flagship restaurant. How apropos that it would come just as he was about to drive over to the Drayson Estate to see his grandmother before heading to Lillian's. Carter crossed out those plans. No way could he look into his grandmother's eyes; she would see straight through him.

The restaurant's offer had been even better than he'd anticipated. Not only would he command a staff of a half dozen pastry chefs and bakers, but he would do so for thirty percent more money than his salary at Lillian's.

Although, it wasn't about the money. It was never about the money.

The most important thing about the conversation he'd just had was the way Grant Robinson had made him feel—as if he would be a valued member of the team. How could someone he'd never met face-to-face make him feel more respected than his own family?

This decision should have been an easy one to make, but it was anything but easy. Carter had something else to consider this time around. Or, rather, some*one* to consider. The thought of leaving for New York didn't have the same appeal it had held just a few weeks ago.

He tried to convince himself that he and Lorraine would be able to handle the distance. New York was just a short plane ride from Chicago, right? The Hawthorne-Hayeses probably owned a private jet. He and Lorraine could make a long-distance relationship work while he gave this new position a shot.

But Carter quickly scratched those plans from his mental idea pad. He could hardly stand to be away from her for a few hours; he couldn't imagine going days or weeks without seeing her. It made his chest ache just to think about it.

When had this happened? How did a woman have him considering changing plans he had been working on even before he'd met her?

He shook his head, letting out a huff of laughter as he thought about how Malik had teased him, and how he'd tried to deny his friend's claims. There wasn't much denying it any longer. He was good and caught. And he didn't want Lorraine to let go anytime soon.

Carter pushed away from the kitchen island and grabbed his keys. An hour later, he found himself sweating under the high-powered lights set up by the photographer in a small area of the kitchen at Lillian's that they had commandeered for today's photo shoot. Even though it was the sweets that were supposed to be on display, Carter felt as if his cheeks were going to break with all the smiling he'd done for the camera.

Drake had hired the photographer to take some preliminary photos for the upcoming *Brothers Who Bake* cookbook. He, Drake and Malik were each sending in two recipes, along with photographs of each step in the baking process. Carter was used to pausing in the middle of baking when he took photos for their Brothers Who Bake blog, but he was never in those photos; it was always just the ingredients.

"How much longer?" Carter asked. Between the heat in the kitchen and the photographer's bright lights, he was sweating like a marathon runner.

"I just need a few more shots of you," the photographer answered. "Let's make these action shots. Pretend you're mixing something in the bowl, or put a pan in the oven, but don't look at the camera."

Carter did as he was told so that he could be done with it all. He wasn't in the right headspace for playing it up for the camera. Or even for baking, for that matter.

That, above all else, told him that the old Carter had indelibly changed. The kitchen was the *first* place he escaped to when he needed to clear his head. There had been several instances in the past when Drake had been forced to send out messages via Lillian's online social networks advertising extra cakes in the bakery because Carter had gone on a baking tear. Something told him that his go-to solution wouldn't cut it this time.

He shook his head. When had a woman ever held such power over him?

It scared the hell out of him to think that she could

influence a decision that was so important to his life, but Carter knew he would not be able to give Grant Robinson an answer until he knew exactly how Lorraine felt about him.

"That went pretty well," Drake said, coming up to him.

Malik followed. "So, once the photographer gets back to us with the pictures, we're going to get together to decide which ones we want to send to the publishers?"

Drake held up a smart card. "I've got the pictures right here. We're going to do that right now."

"I can't," Carter said. "I've got too much to do today."

"Like what?" both Drake and Malik asked in unison.

"Like take care of my own damn business," he bit out.

"We need to get this stuff done now, Carter," Malik pointed out.

"Can't it wait?"

"Until when?" Drake asked. "We have to start preparing for *You Take the Cake* soon, and then we'll all be heading to California in a few weeks."

"I have to—" But Carter stopped. He didn't want either his cousin's or Malik's opinion. The discussion he needed to have would be between himself and Lorraine. Outside influences would only muddy already murky water.

"So, are you in or are you out, Carter?" Malik asked.

"He's in," Drake said. "We can't postpone this."

Carter checked the time on his cell phone. It was already midafternoon. He cursed under his breath.

"I'm in," he said. "Just give me a minute to take care of something."

He sent Lorraine a quick text message, asking if she'd like to have coffee in an hour. She replied seconds later, reminding him that she and her sister were doing pre-wedding shopping today. Carter replied with an invitation for dinner, which she accepted, complete with a smiley face at the end of the text message.

He couldn't stop his grin from forming. Just the simplest gesture from this woman made him so happy it caused a lump of something he'd tried to deny to form in his throat. But he was no longer denying what it was that had captured his heart—his complete soul.

He loved Lorraine Hawthorne-Hayes with the kind of love he'd never thought possible, and he knew she felt the same way about him.

Yes, they had a lot to discuss at dinner tonight. It was one of the most important dinners of his life, because it could possibly change the course of his life. Forever.

Chapter 14

Sitting before the vanity in her bathroom, Lorraine applied just a touch of mascara to her lashes. She had been slowly reducing the amount of makeup she wore because, contrary to popular belief in her usual circle of acquaintances, appearance was not everything. Carter didn't care about how much makeup she wore; he thought she was just as sexy in a pair of jeans and one of his T-shirts, wearing no makeup at all.

Lorraine smiled at her reflection.

She was *so* in love.

And she was no longer afraid.

Yes, she and Carter had only been dating for a few weeks—at dinner tonight they would celebrate their three-week anniversary—but in that short amount of time she had grown closer to him and learned more about him than any other man she'd ever been with before. Carter was everything she could ever hope to find in a man. She could see herself being with him, being this incredibly happy, for…ever.

Lorraine pulled in a shallow, anxious breath.

She didn't want to think in terms of forever. Not yet. Despite how close she and Carter had grown over these past few weeks, it was unwise to have such thoughts this soon.

In the back of her mind was the knowledge that Carter was still contemplating moving to New York. She hated to think of him leaving after her just finding him, but Lorraine knew that this was a decision Carter needed to make for himself. She would complicate his decision even more by divulging just how much he'd come to mean to her in such a short amount of time. It wasn't fair to place that kind of pressure on him.

But, God, how she hoped he felt the same way about her.

He'd told her that he loved her, and she had believed him one hundred percent. But was Carter's idea of love the same as hers?

If there was one thing she had learned in life, it was that one person's concept of love didn't always measure up to someone else's. She would never doubt that her father loved her, but Arnold Hawthorne-Hayes's idea of love was throwing money at his children so that they wouldn't bother him with pesky intangibles, like needing time and attention. Her mother's idea of love was controlling every aspect of Lorraine's life in order to shield her from the world, so that Lorraine would never again find herself in a situation like the one Broderick had created with his blackmail and lies.

What was Carter's idea of love?

Lorraine glanced past the open door, and into her bedroom. Inside the bureau's top drawer was that private investigator's report. How many of the many women listed in there had Carter whispered "I love you" to as he'd held them close? Had he tenderly made love to all of them in that warm, inviting bed of his? Was that what he considered love?

"Stop it," Lorraine demanded. She'd made the choice to ignore what the P.I. had written, and she was sticking to it. For all she knew, everything within the pages of that report had been made up. She wouldn't put anything past her mother.

She went over to her dresser to get her simple pearl studs. On the bureau was a blank printout of the form for the arts fellowship she'd applied for, the one her father had ripped up. She had printed another form the very next day, but had yet to fill it out and submit it.

"I'll get to it tomorrow," she promised herself.

She grabbed her earrings and put them in, then opened the top drawer and pulled out a pair of panties. She slipped the extra pair of underwear in her purse.

A few weeks ago, she would have blushed just at the thought of bringing extra panties on a date, but she'd grown by leaps and bounds in this short amount of time. She'd allowed shame over those pictures Broderick had taken to stifle her body's needs for far too long. She was done feeling ashamed about pursuing sexual pleasure. She was a young, healthy, vibrant woman, and thanks to Carter, she knew what she wanted when it came to her sexuality.

She headed for the kitchen so she could let Frannie know that she might not be back tonight. Lorraine stopped short when she found her mother standing in the middle of the kitchen instead.

"Mother, I thought you had flown to San Diego with Father."

"I changed my mind at the last minute," her mother said. "Actually, this changed my mind for me."

Her mother motioned to a flat brown envelope sitting on the kitchen countertop.

"If that's about Carter, you can keep it," Lorraine said. "Nothing that investigator says will change the way I feel about him."

"Really?" Her mother's brows rose as she opened the flap on the envelope and pulled out a single photograph. "Would seeing it with your own eyes change anything?"

Lorraine braced herself as her mother flipped the photograph over. She had expected to see Carter in the throes of passion with another woman—or worse, more than one woman in the same bed. Instead, her brow furrowed as she stared at a group photo of young men, at least fifty, standing in front of a large house with tall white columns.

"What is this?" Lorraine asked, taking the picture from her mother. "Is this a fraternity photo?"

"Yes," her mother answered. "Your new boyfriend is in the front row, the last person on the left. Did you know Carter belonged to a fraternity?"

Lorraine gave an indifferent shrug as she found Carter. He looked so much younger. He couldn't have been more than eighteen or nineteen in this picture.

"He mentioned that he joined the fraternity that his father belonged to during his one year of college. He said it was one of the main reasons he started at a regular four-year college, even though he knew he wanted to go to culinary school." She looked up at her mother. "What difference does this make? Father is a member of a fraternity. So is Stuart."

"Would you care to learn who else is in that fraternity?" her mother asked. "Look at the top row, the third person from the right."

Lorraine looked where her mother had directed, and her blood turned to ice.

"Is this…?"

"Broderick Collins." Her mother said the name that Lorraine couldn't force herself to utter. "Don't you think it's interesting that Carter and Broderick were in the same fraternity?"

An unbearable tightness constricted her lungs, making it nearly impossible to breathe.

"This…" She started, but had to stop. Her throat ached, clogged with a knot of anxiety that refused to dissipate. She swallowed and tried again. "This doesn't mean anything," she finally managed to get out, though her voice was so weak she barely heard the words.

"You don't believe that." It was a statement from her mother, not a question. "You know exactly what this means."

"Please, don't say anymore."

"You are not this blind, Lorraine."

"Carter did not seek me out, Mother. If I had not gone into Lillian's to order Trina's cake, I would never have met him. He didn't even know who I was at the time."

"Or maybe he knew exactly who you were, and pretended not to, because he remembered that his fraternity brother was able to swindle a million dollars from the Hawthorne-Hayeses."

Lorraine shook her head. "Carter would never do that," she said, cursing her voice for remaining so weak. "You don't know him."

"No, you're the one who doesn't know him. You are holding the proof in your hands, Lorraine. Are you really going to stand there and tell me that you don't think he knew *exactly* who you were?"

Lorraine stood straight, holding herself as rigid as possible as she faced her mother's blistering stare. "I have to go. I'm meeting Carter for dinner," she said.

She could feel the rage radiating from her mother. It flowed from her in a pulsing wave of disapproval, but Lorraine ignored it. Abigail had dictated her life for far too long. Only now did she see just how much of herself she'd relinquished to her mother.

But, try as she might, Lorraine couldn't ignore the sickening feeling that settled in her stomach, or the chill that raced along her skin at seeing Broderick Collins's face again.

Most disturbing of all was seeing him standing only a few yards from Carter.

She returned to her room and sat on the edge of the bed. Lorraine concentrated on taking slow, deep breaths in an attempt to calm the rapid beating of her heart.

They were fraternity brothers. How could Carter *not* have known Broderick?

Her mother's warnings roared back to life, taunting her. They were joined by memories of that awful scene that had taken place five years ago, when her father had called her into his office and confronted her with those photos. She recalled with amazing alacrity the absolute horror she'd experienced as she'd stared at pictures of her completely nude, twenty-year-old self, mimicking the suggestive poses of models in *Playboy* magazines she'd found in Stuart's room.

Lorraine closed her eyes against the shame that washed over her, even five years later. It had taken months before she could look either of her parents in the eye. She had never known such complete humiliation. Yet it didn't hold a candle to the mortification she would have faced if Broderick had made good on his threat and released those photos.

Had Carter known about that? Had he seen the pictures? Had they been passed around the frat house so all of the fraternity brothers could ogle and laugh at the silly little rich girl Broderick had conned into stripping nude for him?

Lorraine clutched her stomach, the pain causing her to double over.

There was only one way to find out if Carter knew of her before that day she'd met him at Lillian's three weeks ago.

Taking a few moments to collect herself before rising from the bed, she stalked back into the kitchen and snatched the envelope from the counter. On the short drive to the restaurant, she tried to calm her frayed nerves so that she could think clearly.

She wanted to give Carter the benefit of the doubt. The picture was damning evidence, but it wasn't proof that he had somehow collaborated with Broderick to make a fool out of her. However, when she pieced together other things she'd read in the P.I. report, Lorraine didn't like the story it created.

Could a renowned ladies' man suddenly fall head over heels for a woman he barely knew? That was exactly what had happened to her—she had fallen for him—but she had to be realistic. Her few past relationships had taught her that most men had another agenda when it came to dating her.

Had she only seen what she'd wanted to see in Carter? Had he been making a fool out of her this entire time?

A better question was, what did he want from her?

And what was he willing to do to get it?

* * *

Carter pulled up to the valet at Les Nomades and hopped out of the car. He slipped the guy a fifty and raced into the restaurant. He was nearly a half hour late. He'd texted Lorraine to let her know that he'd been caught up at the bakery longer than he'd planned to be, but she hadn't responded. Carter hoped she was running late, too.

"I have a reservation for two for Carter Drayson," he told the maître d'.

"Yes, Mr. Drayson. The other person in your party is already here."

Carter grimaced, hating that he'd kept her waiting. He was shown to the same table he and Lorraine had shared on their first date three weeks ago. Her back was turned to him. Carter walked up to her and placed a kiss on that soft, fragrant spot behind her ear. She stiffened beneath his lips.

"Sorry for startling you," he said as he took the seat across the table from her and accepted a menu from the server. "And I'm sorry I'm late. Drake and Malik had me tied up all day with that photo shoot for the *Brothers Who Bake* cookbook. Thankfully, Drake has taken the lead on this. He's working with a writer to get the proposal in order and shipped off to the publisher."

At her complete silence, Carter looked up from his menu. "I'll shut up now. You probably don't want to hear about all of this."

The silence ensued.

Carter's brow furrowed. "Is everything okay?"

She didn't answer. Instead, she reached for her wine goblet and brought it to her lips.

A fissure of unease stalked down Carter's spine at

her remoteness. He wasn't *that* late. Carter motioned to her wineglass.

"That's a good idea. Is that the merlot?"

"Pinot noir."

Her cold, lifeless voice caused his unease to ratchet up a notch. "Rainey, what's going on?" Carter asked. "Did something happen today? Is it your parents? Your sister?"

She didn't answer, just brought the glass to her lips again. But then she set the wine back on the table without taking a sip. She cleared her throat, and finally met his gaze directly.

"Do you know someone by the name of Broderick Collins?" she asked, her voice soft, hollow.

Carter frowned. He shook his head. "I don't think so." He sensed that he'd answered wrong. Disappointment instantly clouded her eyes, and she expelled a sad sigh.

"Should I know him?" he asked.

Lorraine reached down under the table and came up with a brown envelope. She pulled out a picture and set it on the table.

He instantly recognized the scene, even though he hadn't laid eyes on the group photo he'd taken in front of the fraternity house in at least nine years. He'd had a copy once, but Carter had been so far removed from that world for so long, he wouldn't be surprised if he'd tossed it out years ago.

"Where did you get this?" Carter asked.

She didn't answer his question, just said, "Broderick is on the top row, the third from the right."

Carter picked out the guy, but still didn't remember him. "Lorraine, I don't get—"

"He is the person who blackmailed my family for a million dollars," she said softly.

Carter's eyes shot to hers. "Lorraine, you can't think—" But he didn't get a chance to even finish his statement before she pushed back from the table and ran out of the restaurant.

"Shit." Carter took off after her, not giving a damn that their hasty exit drew stares from several tables. "Lorraine," he called. He looked down the street and saw her walking toward Fairbanks Court. Carter made it to her in five strides.

"Lorraine, what in the hell is going on here? Where did you even get that picture?" He caught her by the shoulder, halting her escape. "Would you talk to me?"

She turned and crossed her arms over her chest. She looked so small, so vulnerable.

So lost.

Carter wanted to gather her into his arms and pretend that the past five minutes had been some type of nightmare. At the same time he wanted to lash out at her. What she was accusing him of was unthinkable.

Avoiding his eyes, Lorraine said, "My mother hired a private investigator. It was he who discovered that you and Broderick belonged to the same fraternity."

Carter's head snapped back. "You had me investigated?"

Her eyes flashed to his. "It was my mother who had you investigated. Apparently her suspicions were warranted."

"You really think that I'm somehow connected to this Collins guy?" Carter closed his eyes and ran a hand down his face. He could not believe this. "Do you think this has all been some kind of elaborate scheme? You think these past three weeks have been a lie?"

She pressed her lips together, shook her head. She glanced up at him, but quickly averted her gaze.

"I don't know what to think anymore, Carter. The one thing I *do* know is that three weeks ago I had no idea who you were, and you supposedly had no knowledge of me, either."

"I *didn't* know you," he said. "Sure, I knew of your family—who in Chicago hasn't heard of Hawthorne-Hayes Jewelers? But it wasn't until our picture turned up in the paper following our first date that I discovered *you* were a Hawthorne-Hayes."

When she looked up at him, her big brown eyes were filled with accusation. "Did that episode occur by chance, or did the photographer get a tip that we would be at the restaurant?"

Carter's eyes widened. "Are you kidding me?"

"It wouldn't be the first time that I've had something like that happen. I've learned over the years that the people you think you know well can turn out to be the most unscrupulous." She shook her head. "The fact is, Carter, despite the time we've spent together, I really don't know you all that well."

Carter looked around, pretty sure he was being *Punk'd*. He returned his attention to her and held his hands out, pleading for her to consider her accusations, and how they made zero sense.

"Lorraine, do you hear what you're saying? I met you when you came to the bakery to order a cake. If this was all some elaborate scheme, how in the hell would I have orchestrated that? It's not as if I dragged you into Lillian's that day."

She stared off into the distance, as if she wasn't even paying attention.

"Why me?" she asked, bringing her eyes back to his.

"You've been with dozens of women in the past. Why am I the one you've supposedly fallen in love with?"

"What makes you think I've been with *dozens* of women?"

"It was in the report. Apparently, your string of ex-girlfriends—if one could even call them that—are all too willing to talk about Carter Drayson's penchant for loving them and leaving them. What did I do to make you commit to an entire three weeks, and to fall in love, as you claim?"

For a long moment, all Carter could do was stare at her. His lungs constricted, making it hard to breathe. He shook his head, grappling with the mixture of hurt and anger rioting through him.

"You're going to take the word of some guy your mother hired—the same mother you admit has tried to control your every move for the past five years?"

"What would she gain by lying, Carter? My mother is trying to protect me. Although I don't always agree with her tactics, her goal has always been to protect me."

"Your mother is trying to control you," he argued. "And you're allowing her to do it."

"I want to believe you, Carter, but when I put together everything—all the women you've been with, that picture of you and Broderick…" She pressed a hand to her throat, as if it were hard for her to swallow.

Carter dropped his shoulders, defeat sinking into his bones. He saw the uncertainty on her face and it was too much for him to stomach. He'd spent too much of his life trying to prove who he was to people who supposedly loved him. He wasn't up for this fight.

"If that's what you want to believe, Lorraine, I can't stop you." He hunched his shoulders. "I'm just some player with a string of women lined up to take your place. How does that sound?"

This time the hurt that flickered in her eyes didn't affect him. He had his own hurt and disappointment to deal with; he couldn't be concerned with hers.

"Is that true, Carter?"

"That's what your mother wants you to believe, right? She told you that you were just another notch on my belt? Fine, you were just another notch on my belt."

Her bottom lip trembled, and she seemed to fold even more into herself, wrapping her arms around her middle and bending over slightly. Carter had to stop himself from reaching for her.

When she looked up at him, her eyes were filled with so much pain it nearly brought him to his knees.

"You promised you wouldn't turn out to be like all the rest," she accused in a quiet, hurt-filled voice. "You said you wouldn't hurt me."

"Don't blame me for this. I didn't do this. You did. Your mother did." Carter tipped his head up to the sky and let out a mirthless laugh. "When I think about what I had planned to discuss tonight…" When he returned his gaze to Lorraine's pained expression, he couldn't summon a bit of remorse. "I guess this means I'm taking that job in New York. Thanks for making the decision easy for me."

He turned and stalked away from her.

Chapter 15

Lorraine stared unseeingly out the window of her loft. Her brain registered only the muted colors of the outside world, which were dulled even more by the overcast sky. When her gaze came into focus, it homed in on several beads of rain trailing down the pane of glass.

Lorraine quickly averted her eyes. The rain reminded her too much of the tears that had been rolling down her face for the past two days.

She backed away from the window, running her hands up and down her arms in an attempt to ward off the chill in her bones that she couldn't seem to get rid of. She trudged over to the bed, her limbs heavy with the weight of her conflicted emotions.

She didn't know what to think anymore. She didn't know whom to believe. Although she had been appalled at her mother's methods, Lorraine had no doubt that her mother had had her best interest at heart. No, that wasn't true. Abigail had had the interest of the Hawthorne-Hayes family name at heart. Nevertheless, her actions were explainable.

Carter's, on the other hand, were not.

She had been swept up in the fantasy of his attention these past three weeks, yet Lorraine couldn't deny the pesky feelings of doubt that had crept into her mind on several occasions. He'd seemed too good to be true. Now she knew why.

Or did she?

Was it all one big coincidence? Was there a possibility that Carter had had no idea that the man who had blackmailed her family was the same man who had belonged to his fraternity?

Lorraine closed her eyes, trying to recall his face at dinner the other night when he'd looked at the photograph. She'd kept her eyes on his face, hoping to catch any glimpse of recognition. She'd been waiting for that flash of guilt. But there had been none. Did that mean he really didn't know Broderick, or that Carter Drayson was a compelling actor?

She curled up on her bed with a pillow, trying to convince herself that she didn't smell his scent on the linens, and cursing herself for ever bringing him into her most sacred space. Carter had spurred her to do things she'd never considered. He'd motivated her to open up in ways she'd never thought possible.

"How could it have all been a lie?" Lorraine whispered.

Her cell phone trilled, startling her from her melancholy stupor. She recognized the number as one that she'd called earlier today. Lorraine forced herself upright. Pushing aside her mother, Carter, the private investigator and every other negative drain on her emotions, she answered the phone.

"Hello, Mrs. Stanton," she began with a cheerfulness that was completely opposed to what she was actually feeling inside. "Thank you for returning my call. I have an idea I would like to propose for the patients at Comer Children's Hospital and the pediatric burn unit at University of Chicago Medical."

Carter stuffed an extra couple of pairs of boxers into the side compartment of his carry-on, then went into the bathroom to retrieve the toiletry bag that he kept packed. He used to keep it in his car, just in case he found himself spending the night somewhere other than his own home after a long night of clubbing. He remembered the day he'd brought it in from the car, after his second date with Lorraine. After years of playing the field, he'd decided after just two dates with her that his nights of hard partying and casual hookups were over.

Carter let out a long, eloquent string of curse words as he continued packing. He'd ordered himself not to think about her. If Lorraine wanted to believe the worst about him, that was her choice. It wasn't up to him to try to change her mind. He had enough issues on his plate; he wouldn't waste any more of his mental energy thinking about her lack of trust.

Her complete, wholehearted, *revolting* lack of trust.

"Forget about her," Carter bit out.

He needed to erase from his mind what she'd come to mean to him over these past three weeks. Carter knew of one sure way to accomplish that.

He opened the cabinet underneath his sink, grabbed the box of condoms and tossed a handful into his toiletry bag. Best way to get over one girl was to find himself another. Or several. Hell, he'd hook up with half the women in New York if that was what it took to prove that he was over Lorraine.

A ball of nausea settled like a lead anchor at the sight of the foil packets. Carter emptied everything from the bag onto his counter, plucking the condoms and dumping them in the trash.

Random sex with random women wouldn't solve a damn thing. It never had in the past. In fact, it probably had a lot to do with how screwed up he was when it came to relationships.

"Relationships?" he snorted.

He didn't *do* relationships. He didn't even know how. These past three weeks with Lorraine had been the closest thing he'd ever experienced to a real relationship, and it had all just blown up in his face.

It was time he face the inevitable. He was thirty years old, and like his father, he was well on his way to living a life filled with one-night stands separated by stretches of long, lonely days.

Carter sat on the rim of his tub and cradled his head in his hands.

He didn't want to follow in his father's footsteps. He needed more. After that morsel of happiness he'd found with Lorraine, Carter had quickly begun to crave the taste of it. He wanted to savor that feeling every day for the rest of his life.

Like a fool, he'd allowed himself to picture a future with her. Finally, he'd begun to see himself as more than just the bastard Drayson grandson, more than the black sheep who was merely tolerated by the rest of the family. When Lorraine looked at him with those soulful brown eyes, he saw reflected in them the man he'd always hoped he could one day become. He saw a man who deserved the love of a good woman.

But she didn't love him. Carter refused to believe that she could love him yet believe him capable of something as heinous as colluding with that bastard who'd blackmailed her.

"Forget about her," Carter said with more force. This time, he meant it.

He grabbed his phone from the bathroom counter and called Malik.

"Hey, man," Malik answered.

"Do you have everything you need?" Carter asked him.

Carter had only been responsible for one specialty cake order for this weekend, which he'd finished decorating earlier this morning. But he always had contingencies in place just in case any of his customers needed an emergency cake.

"I've got a handle on everything," Malik answered. "Although I still don't think you should get on that plane."

He'd been over this with Malik, and frankly, he was tired of hearing his best friend's opinion.

"I'm not discussing this again," he said. "I have an eight-thirty return flight scheduled out of JFK for tomorrow night. Text me if anything pops up that needs my attention."

"So, you're worried about the place falling apart with you gone for one day? How can you justify leaving forever?"

That feeling of nausea climbed up his throat again. Carter tamped it down, refusing to succumb to the guilt that had been eating away at him from the moment he'd first entertained talks with Robinson Restaurants.

"I'll talk to you when I get back," he said, then disconnected the call before Malik had a chance to respond.

He wasn't doing this to hurt Lillian's. He was doing this to help himself. He was done being underappreciated, sacrificing his own career without getting anything in return. It was time that he put himself first. It was time for a fresh start.

New York would be that fresh start.

Carter repacked his toiletry bag, leaving the discarded condoms in the garbage. He dropped the toiletry bag into the carry-on, turned off all the lights in his condo and headed out the door.

Chapter 16

Carter tapped a nervous rhythm on the crisp white linen as his eyes roamed over the tasteful, yet understated decor of Robinson Restaurants's flagship location in Midtown Manhattan. From what he'd read, the proprietor, Grant Robinson, believed in keeping his restaurants simple and elegant, because the food spoke for itself.

And he wanted Carter's desserts to become a part of that proud tradition. It was humbling. And exciting. And just a bit overwhelming.

It wasn't until he was strapping himself into his seat on the airplane at O'Hare that the reality of what he would face had dawned on him. His cakes would have to stand on their own. They would no longer be backed by the reputation Lillian's had built.

"Carter?"

He popped up from his seat and turned to face the man holding out his hand.

The man introduced himself. "Grant Robinson."

"Carter Drayson," he said, shaking Grant's hand. He was immediately taken aback. Something about Grant Robinson's green eyes looked eerily familiar.

"How was the flight from Chicago?" Grant asked as he unbuttoned the single closure on his jacket and took the seat across from Carter.

"Quick and easy," Carter answered.

"I guess that's a good thing. I'm sure you'll be taking frequent trips back home to visit family. Everyone still lives around that Drayson Estate in Glenville Heights, right?" he asked with a smile.

Carter's head popped back with shock. He'd seen Grant Robinson's dimpled smile before. Something downright crazy was going on here.

"Carter?"

Dammit, he had to pull it together. He was blowing the hell out of this interview.

"Uh, I'm sorry," he said, shaking his head. "Yes, all of my family is back in Chicago. How do you know about my family's estate?"

A ghost of a grin traced across Grant's lips. "I didn't mention this in any of our previous conversations, but I went to college with your cousin Shari."

Comprehension nearly knocked Carter out of his chair.

That was where he'd seen that smile and those green eyes.

Andre.

This man looked exactly like his cousin Shari's four-year-old son.

Carter reached for the glass of water the waitress

had set before him and downed half of it in one gulp. "So, you knew Shari back in the day, huh?" he asked.

Grant nodded. "But enough about that. Why don't we get to the reason you're really here? As I've mentioned in our previous phone conversations, I think someone with your skill set and experience would be an excellent addition to Robinson Restaurants."

As the man imparted all the ways in which Carter and Robinson Restaurants were a perfect fit, Carter could only think about the many instances he'd sensed something deep and dark lurking behind Shari's usually bright smile. His cousin had been keeping this secret from the world, and certainly from Andre's father.

Carter shook his head to clear it. He pushed aside Shari's dilemma and concentrated on what Grant Robinson was saying.

"Lillian's has a reputation for creating some of the best baked goods in the entire state of Illinois. I know that you have had much to do with the bakery garnering that reputation in the last few years."

Carter let out a self-deprecating laugh. "I can't take that much credit," he said. "My grandmother is the one who built the business. Much of what I know, I learned from her. Culinary school just helped me to hone what she'd taught all of us while growing up in the bakery."

"She taught you well. I'm sure she's very proud of the entire Drayson clan."

Carter pulled in a deep breath. "Yes. She is."

And his leaving would undoubtedly break his grandmother's heart.

"So, what do you say, Carter? Have I convinced you to take what you've learned at Lillian's and bring it to the Big Apple?"

Carter fidgeted with the silverware at his place setting. He picked up his water glass, took a sip, set it down and then picked it up again. He was stalling.

But not anymore.

He looked Grant Robinson in the eye. "When would I have to start?"

Carter pulled into his parking spot at his condo, but instead of getting out of the car, he sat behind the wheel and stared straight ahead at the concrete wall. He'd been nursing the tight ache in his chest since the moment he'd concluded his phone call with Grant Robinson over an hour ago—a phone call he'd made after leaving his grandparents' home.

He'd made up his mind while still sitting across the table from Robinson back at his restaurant last Saturday night, yet for an entire week Carter had weighed the pros and cons, debated, questioning whether the choice he'd made was the right one.

In the end, Carter knew he'd chosen the only option that could truly make him happy.

It was done. Decision made. It was time for him to stop lamenting over it and start on the path forward.

He got out of the car. Carter opted for the stairs up to his apartment. He stopped short when he rounded the corner and spotted a figure standing in front of his door.

"Lorraine?"

She let out a yelp and turned, clutching her chest with her free hand. "Goodness, Carter. You scared me."

"What are you doing here?" Carter checked his watch. "It's after eleven o'clock."

He walked the rest of the way to the door, but stopped a couple of feet away from her.

"I went looking for you at the bakery today. Your friend Malik said that you were visiting your grandparents, letting them know your decision regarding the job in New York. I decided to wait for you."

"What do you want?" Carter asked, trying to ignore the ache that settled in his gut just at the sight of her. It had only been a week since he'd last seen her, yet it felt as if it had been a year.

"May I...?" She paused for a moment. "May I come in?"

Despite the quiet confidence in her voice, there was a vulnerability clouding her eyes that struck his chest with the force of a mallet. He had to remind himself that he hadn't done anything wrong here.

Carter stared at her for several moments. He didn't trust himself to move. If he did, he wouldn't be able to fight this compulsion to assuage the hurt that was so evident in her once bright eyes. He wanted to take her into his arms and wrap them around her; instead, he put one of his hands in his pocket and used the other to open the door to his condo.

For a second, Carter contemplated closing the door behind him. It would be easier all around if she just went home. But she'd made the effort to come here. The least he could do was hear her out.

With a quick nod, he gestured for her to come in. She didn't look at him as she entered the apartment, and once inside, she walked over to the far side of the kitchen island, as if she needed to put some distance between them.

It pissed him off.

"Do you think I would actually put a hand on you?" Carter bit out.

"No." She shook her head. "No, of course not, Carter. I know you would never hurt me."

"Really? It sounds as if you've changed your tune since the last time we talked."

"Perhaps I deserve that," she said. She straightened her shoulders, as if shoring up her courage. "I had several reasons for wanting to see you. I'm asking that you hear me out."

"I can't make any promises. Though you probably wouldn't believe any promise I made anyway."

The hurt that flashed across her face made Carter instantly want to take back his words. She hadn't come in hurling more accusations. There was no justification for his cruelty toward her.

Despite his unwarranted callousness, Lorraine continued in that same poised, self-assured manner.

"First, I wanted to apologize for my mother's actions. She saw nothing wrong with hiring that private investigator, but it wasn't right."

"Yet you still believe everything he had to say."

"Second," she continued as if he'd never spoken, "I want to apologize for jumping to conclusions after reading his report. It was only later that I realized that picture was taken over a decade ago, five years before I ever met Broderick. You had already left college by that time. You once told me that you'd given up the fraternity life a long time ago, so it isn't unreasonable to deduce that you did not keep in touch with people from the fraternity."

That thought hadn't even occurred to him.

"If we had been in a court of law, everything that investigator brought forth would have been considered circumstantial evidence," Lorraine continued. "I allowed the things I'd read to cloud my judgment, but I now realize that I should not have left without first discussing it with you."

Carter felt a tiny spark of hope blossom in his chest and cursed himself for yielding even that small amount. Her apology wasn't enough to erase what she'd done to him when she'd pulled out that picture and accused him of duplicity. She'd devastated him. How did he know she wouldn't do it again the next time her mother sought to "protect" her?

"Those are only words, Lorraine."

"Yes, they are," she said. "Words are all I can offer. I was wrong, and I know that I hurt you. I'm sorry for that. I hope you can accept my apology."

He folded his arms across his chest. "What if I can't?"

She flinched, breaking eye contact for a moment.

"That is…understandable," she said in a more subdued tone. She pulled in a shaky breath. "There was one more reason for my visit. I wanted to thank you."

Carter's eyes shot to hers.

"Movers were at my parents' home today, packing up my things. I'm moving to my loft until I can find something more permanent. Also, on Monday, I'm holding my first art class at Comer Children's Hospital. I will be teaching there and at the burn unit twice a week. Neither of those things would have happened if not for you, so I wanted to thank you."

Carter shook his head. "I don't deserve credit for that."

"Yes, you do." She nodded. "I should have moved out of my parents' home a long time ago. But I stayed, thinking that the freedom I gave up was a small price to pay in return for the security they provided. I know now that I can stand on my own. As for the hospital… well, let's just say that once I saw you with those children, several things became clear."

Carter studied her, struck by the self-assuredness she

exuded. He tried to recall that reserved, timid woman who'd walked into Lillian's to order a cake for her sister's bridal shower. He could barely picture her; that was just how much confidence she had acquired.

"What became clear?" he asked.

"Carter, before I met you I was lost. I knew I wanted to do more, but I didn't know what, if anything, I could contribute, other than writing a check from the Hawthorne-Hayes Foundation. The night of the event at Lincoln Park Zoo, I realized that there was a way for me to give back. After we visited the hospital, and I saw Delaney's sketches, I knew I'd found it."

She took several steps forward, stopping a few feet from him. "So, thank you," she said. "And goodbye."

Carter fisted his hands against the cold granite of the kitchen island as he listened to the hollow sound of her footsteps as she made her way toward the door. He pinched his eyes shut, felt a muscle jumping in his jaw as it clenched in angry resentment.

"I want to know why," he said in a quiet voice.

Her footsteps halted.

Carter turned. To her back, he said, "In the time we were together, what had I ever done to make you think I was capable of doing what you accused me of, Lorraine?"

Finally, she turned. Her chin dipped for just a moment before she brought her head up and looked him directly in the eye.

"It had nothing to do with you, Carter. It was about me, and what I had come to expect." She paused, rubbing her hands up and down her arms. After a moment she dropped her hands and brought her gaze back to his, that silent strength returning.

"A month ago, when I accepted that first dinner invitation from you, it was the boldest and scariest thing I had done in years," she said. "Those first few days, it felt as if I was a different person, some actor pretending to be this woman who flirted and kissed a man on the first date. But then I started to realize that the person I'd allowed myself to become—this aloof, unapproachable person—was the real fraud."

She pointed to her chest. "This person, the one you helped me to rediscover—this is the real Lorraine."

"I'd fallen in love with the real Lorraine," Carter said quietly. "You don't know what it took for me to say those three words to you. I'd never said them to another woman."

The look of anguish that crossed her face ripped at Carter's heart. She pulled her quivering bottom lip between her teeth.

"I have never loved someone the way I love you, Rainey. I didn't think love could happen that fast, not the deep love I found myself feeling. But it did. And then you throw me in the same boat with the bastard that blackmailed you, all because of a picture that was taken nearly ten years ago. Do you know what that did to me?"

He drew a frustrated hand down his face.

"I only joined that fraternity because my dad and uncle were a part of it, but I knew from early on that it just wasn't me. I didn't take the time to get to know anyone there. The day that picture was taken, I showed up to the frat house, was there for the five minutes it took the photographer to snap the photo and I left. I don't remember ever meeting Broderick Collins, and I've *never* had any dealings with him."

"Carter, please try to see things from my perspective. At the time, all I had to go on was the evidence sitting right in front of me, and my mother's warnings ringing in my ears, telling me that you were making a fool of me."

"But—" Carter started, but she stopped him.

"No, please. You need to understand this." She folded her arms across her chest, rubbing her hands over her forearms as if warding off a chill. Her voice, when she continued, was muted. "What happened with Broderick has haunted me every single day for the past five years. It has controlled my life in more ways than my mother ever could." She looked up at him. "You showed me that it doesn't have as much power over me as I thought it did. You showed me that my past mistakes do not have to define my future."

"So why did you let it?" he asked, running an agitated hand through his hair.

"Because it's what I had become used to. Don't you get it, Carter?" She held her hands out, as if pleading with him to understand. "I didn't know how to be happy. I didn't think I deserved it. That's my ugly truth. As amazing as these past few weeks with you have been, a part of me has been waiting for the other shoe to drop, for the joy I'd found to be snatched away from me.

"When my mother handed me her so-called proof, in a way, I felt justified, as if it was nothing more than what I had expected to happen all along."

"So you're telling me that this entire time you've just been waiting for me to break your heart?"

She lifted her shoulders in a hapless shrug. "I thought it was inevitable," she said, the words coming out ragged, clogged with emotion. She pushed out a weary sigh. "And in the end, it was a self-fulfilling prophecy. I figured out a way to get my heart broken on my own. I thought I was more prepared for it this time around, but it seems that the harder you love, the greater the hurt."

The words clutched at Carter's heart, squeezing it like a giant fist. He'd felt that kind of love, and knew that kind of hurt.

Lorraine straightened her shoulders, and drew in a shattering breath.

"Thank you for allowing me the opportunity to apologize. I didn't want you to leave for New York believing that I still thought you were guilty."

He had to swallow several times before he was able to speak. Finally, he asked, "What changed your mind about me?"

"Other than the fact that the timeline doesn't match up?" she asked. She tilted her head to the side, a somber smile touching her lips. "It was something I told my mother from the very beginning. You and Broderick are nothing alike. I know the type of person you are, Carter. You have shown me your heart. It's not capable of such treachery."

With a brief nod, she turned and started for the door.

Carter swallowed hard, closing his eyes tight. The lump of emotion clogging his throat felt as big as a baseball. He heard the soft click of the doorknob turn as she opened it.

"Don't leave," he managed to get out. He opened his eyes. Lorraine stood with her back to him, her hand still on the knob.

"Don't leave," Carter said again.

She turned. A mixture of hope, regret and uncertainty glistened in her expressive brown eyes.

"If you know what's in my heart," he said, "then you know better than to think I would let you walk out of here."

In two strides he was standing before her, mere inches separating their bodies. Carter brought his hand up and caressed her warm cheek, just as a single tear escaped and trailed down her face.

"Carter, I am so sorry," she whispered.

"Never believe that you don't deserve happiness, Rainey. If there is anyone in this world who deserves to be happy, it's you."

She looked up at him, her eyes brimming with tears.

"Do I deserve *you?*" she asked. Her soft palm cupped his jaw. His eyes slid shut, savoring the feel of her. "Say that I deserve you, Carter."

"We deserve each other," he said before dipping his head and capturing her mouth in a slow kiss. Everything in his world fell into place the moment his lips touched hers. Each doubt faded with every swipe of his tongue as it plunged in and out of her sweet, warm mouth. Everything he could ever want was standing right here, wrapped in his arms.

"I love you," Carter breathed into her. "With every single part of me, I love every single part of you."

"I thought I'd never hear you say those words to me again," she whispered. She rested her forehead against his, and looking into his eyes, said, "I love you, too, Carter. With every single part of me."

He kissed her again, long and slow and deep. He had suffered through an entire week of not tasting her lips; it had been the hardest week of his life. With a certainty that reached to the depths of his soul, Carter knew he would never go this long without her again. Not if he wanted to survive.

He finally released her lips but kept his arms around her. He needed to feel her against him. Forever.

Lorraine lowered her head to his chest, resting her cheek against the place where his heart beat.

"I suppose I will begin earning quite a few frequent-flier miles," she said.

"You don't need to fly to Michigan Avenue, do you?"

Her head popped up. "But I thought—"

"I didn't take the job," he said. "I belong at Lillian's. That bakery is a part of me. It's my family."

"Lillian's is lucky to have you," she said.

"I'm just as lucky to have it, and the rest of my family. I'm lucky to have you, too."

"We're lucky to have each other."

With a smile, Carter lowered his head and found heaven in her kiss.

Epilogue

Lorraine tucked the silk sheet more firmly underneath her arms as she sat up in bed. Dozens of papers were strewn across her lap. She had forms for several grants she was applying for that would benefit Comer Children's Hospital. For once, she had no problem throwing around the Hawthorne-Hayes name, especially if it meant more money for the hospital.

She stumbled over the application for the fellowship she'd applied for several weeks ago—the one her father had ripped apart in front of her. Back then she'd thought that earning the fellowship would provide the validation that she had been seeking. Lorraine stared at the paper, then balled it up and tossed it aside.

Carter came around the dividing wall in her loft carrying a coffee mug in one hand and a fluted ramekin in the other. He was bare-chested, and he looked good enough to eat.

He set the mug on the table next to the bed. Taking a seat on the edge of the mattress, he picked up the crumpled paper she'd just tossed.

"What's this?"

"Something I thought I needed," Lorraine said. "But I don't. Not anymore."

Carter shrugged and tossed it with the other forms scattered around the room. He scooted closer to her and spooned a helping of the ramekin's contents. Holding the spoon out to her, he said, "Tell me this crème brûlée isn't the best thing you've ever tasted."

"Crème brûlée for breakfast, Carter?"

He shrugged. "It's time for dessert somewhere in the world. Now open up."

Lorraine shook her head, but obliged. "Mmm…"

"Good, right?"

"Wonderful."

"Better than the one at Les Nomades?"

She pulled her bottom lip between her teeth. "Goodness, look at all the paperwork I have to complete." Carter let out a groan, and she fell into a fit of giggles. "I'm only teasing you. It is the best crème brûlée in the entire world."

"You're just saying that so I'll stop trying."

"Yes, I am, but I know that won't stop you."

"Damn right," he said. He set the ramekin on the table next to her coffee mug and climbed over her on the bed. He sat up against the headboard and pulled her into his arms. "I'm going to perfect that recipe, even if I have to buy every egg yolk in Chicago."

Lorraine belted out a laugh. "I'll alert the area chickens." She nestled closer to him, her naked back against his solid, equally naked chest. "Is there anything special on your agenda today?" she asked.

"I'm heading to the bakery as soon as I can tear myself away from you," Carter replied, kissing her bare shoulder and sending shivers up her spine. "The entire Drayson clan will be there today. It's one of our last meetings before heading to L.A. for *You Take the Cake*." He let out a sigh. "We've got a lot riding on this show, Rainey. We really need this to go off without a hitch."

"It will," she said. "Don't worry."

He shook his head. "I don't know. I have a feeling that some family secrets may not remain a secret for much longer."

"Why so cryptic, Carter?" she said absently, grabbing another grant form.

He tightened his arms around her waist. "I may have inadvertently stumbled across something in New York that I wasn't supposed to know. It explains a lot about something that's been bothering me about my cousin Shari."

His voice held a note of unease that had Lorraine twisting around to face him. "Is it something serious? Is Shari in trouble?"

He peered down at her, and Lorraine realized that the sheet covering her breasts had fallen. Carter's eyes instantly heated.

"It's nothing Shari can't deal with on her own. Besides," he said, pulling the covers completely away from her and tossing them onto the floor. "I'm about to give you all you can handle."

* * * * *

Two classic Eaton novels in one special volume...

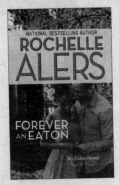

FOREVER
AN EATON
NATIONAL BESTSELLING AUTHOR
ROCHELLE ALERS

In *Bittersweet Love,* a tragedy brings history teacher Belinda Eaton and attorney Griffin Rice closer when they must share custody of their twin goddaughters. Can their partnership turn into a loving relationship that is powerful enough to last?

In *Sweet Deception,* law professor Myles Eaton has struggled for ten years to forget the woman he swore he'd love forever—Zabrina Cooper And just when Myles is sure he's over her, Zabrina arrives back in town As secrets are revealed, can they recapture their incredible, soul-deep chemistry?

"Smoking-hot love scenes, a fascinating story and extremely likable characters combine in a thrilling book that's hard to put down." —RT Book Reviews on SWEET DREAMS

Available May 2013 wherever books are sold!

KPRA 12605

REQUEST YOUR FREE BOOKS!

2 FREE NOVELS PLUS 2 FREE GIFTS!

KIMANI
ROMANCE
™

Love's ultimate destination!

KROM13R